RADIO TEL AVIV

Radio Tel Aviv

Edward Evans

A musical confession by Dr Israel Shine,
translated by Edward Evans

SilverWood

Published in 2018 by SilverWood Books

SilverWood Books Ltd
14 Small Street, Bristol, BS1 1DE, United Kingdom
www.silverwoodbooks.co.uk

ISBN 978-1-78132-787-6 (hardback)
ISBN 978-1-78132-780-7 (paperback)
ISBN 978-1-78132-781-4 (ebook)

British Library Cataloguing in Publication Data
A CIP catalogue record for this book is available from the British Library

Page design and typesetting by SilverWood Books
Printed on responsibly sourced paper

To Liora. My Light. I'm sorry.

Contents

My House Facing the Golan, Arik Einstein

I wanted to touch the sky, but on my seventh birthday, my father said, "It's impossible." As compensation for the cosmic disappointment, I got a radio, and he explained that the music rippled through the universe on invisible waves. Later that week, school finished early, and I turned on the radio that I carried with me in the front pocket of my backpack and left the dirt track by a bright yellow pipe and a bag of cement that had been rained on and transformed into something like the rocks by the ridge by the water. The sky, close at hand, was impossible to touch, but I could feel the radio waves. I couldn't see them, but I could hear them. Arik Einstein sang, "Yet my eyes once again seek the Golan."

The back door of my house was locked. I picked a blade of grass from a crack in the concrete by the flower pot and watched it kite towards the fleeing clouds and down to the Sea of Galilee. The illusion flattened when it hit my sandal. I climbed on a breeze block and got my nose to the window sill. Through the dusty glass, I caught sight of my mother's dress tugged above her hips, her white thighs wobbling and her back arched to the ponytail my father was tugging, her eyes half-lidded, cheeks pink, hair dripping sweat.

She appeared to be muttering, the way she did over candles on Friday night, or when threatening to eat the freckle on the back of my neck. My father's rear pumped, and she shook her head, and his arm reached down. She looked like she was in pain and there came the words that I later dreamt: "*Ich komme, mein Gott, ich bin verdammt ko...*"[1] Her lips crept into a smile, and I stumbled back.

A hot wind dusted the escarpment. My eyes watered as I ran down a steep, rutted path, Arik Einstein singing inside my backpack as if nothing had happened. Now you know why I couldn't stand his music. His voice brought back the memory of my parents having sex. I turned my shoulder, to budge the radio, and tripped. My backpack struck a boulder. I grappled with the zipper and found the radio's volume knob had been knocked off. Blood leaked from my knee to my ankle, but I stood up and kept going. I stopped by the palms, near my grandmother's house, at the edge of the kibbutz, worried that the old women playing bridge would be there. They liked to ruffle my blonde hair. Never mind, I had to fix the volume knob on my radio and deal with my knee.

I opened the back door, limping from the fall. "Who's there?" my grandmother said.

"Me," I said.

"Oy," my grandfather said.

I helped press cotton wool against the cut while my grandmother put on a plaster and said, "What have you done?" I'd always been able to tell her everything, but I couldn't tell her what I'd seen through the window.

"Strawberry jam?" my grandfather said.

"Hate strawberries."

"I know. Here's your toast," he said.

I admired the radio my grandparents never listened to,

a giant device that reflected lamplight in its polished oak and sat like a raven on the mantelpiece, with a pear-shaped dial for a beak. I wondered, but never asked, why it got such a prominent perch. I suspected there was a secret to its silence. Taking down a book from its side, I attempted to decipher the foreign letters on the cover, "*Das Tierreich*," and opening it near the middle, found a picture of a monkey with its mouth wide open and sharp teeth: "*Makaken sind sehr territorial.*"

"What's this language?" I asked.

"German," my grandmother said, lifting her head from her crossword and making a spitting sound – "Tfu!" – while I tried to get my mouth wide open like the monkey's. "You're a good boy. Not a know-it-all like your mother. She thinks she knows what makes us tick. We're not watches. You can't play with our cogs. Stop it, you fool."

My grandfather was putting on a limp and with breath like baked apples said, "I may be a fool, but I fixed your radio." I twizzled the volume knob, thanked them both and set off home. Crickets filled the laurel air and I avoided the music stations, in case Arik Einstein was singing. Panting up the slope, I listened to an announcement that a man called Eichmann was in Jerusalem. The Sea of Galilee was a bottomless black and I was breathless and sweaty by the time I reached the ridge. There was nothing out there but radio waves bringing vague news of a deeper darkness. The back door was propped open by the breeze block, and my mother was stirring a steaming pot, and my father was sitting in a chair reading a journal. "Monkeys," I said.

My father cleared his throat. "Did you know Schubert was thirty-one when he died? Switch off that radio, Israel. I wish I'd never bought it."

11

"You look like a *makaken*," I said.

"Are you speaking German?" my father said.

"And you're a know-it-all."

My mother touched my knee. "What happened?"

"Can I sleep in your bed tonight?"

We ate chicken schnitzel and white beans in silence. After dinner, I went to my bedroom with my radio and listened to more tales from Jerusalem. The door creaked open, and I watched my father's groping shadow approach my feet. "You awake boy?" I pretended to sleep, and he pinched my big toe. "Boy? If you can hear me, do as I say. Go to your mother, she's waiting for you. I'll stay here tonight. And switch that off."

I ran down the corridor, and my mother pulled back the duvet and, getting in, I told myself that I didn't need to tell her what I'd seen that afternoon, but found myself saying, "Sorry."

"What for?"

I thought about what I'd heard on the radio. "Nothing," I said.

Too Much in Love to Hear, The Churchills

There's an absence at our centre like the spark-gap in a radio, a universe inside that I tried to fill with love. I'm sorry, Ori, in the end it didn't work, you see, I'm sitting here all alone, in our apartment on Trumpeldor Street across the road from the cemetery. Resting my scarred arm on my battered copy of *Father of Radio*, I'm writing this memoir using that laptop you bought me, my ghostly reflection behind the words on the screen.

Another sunny day in Tel Aviv, but without you I feel like a shadow. Liora's on your gravestone, but you were Ori to me, my light.[2] All I can do without you is write. I want to explain the things that drove me mad. Did I ever tell you that Heinrich Hertz inherited granulomatosis from his father and that his bust was removed from its alcove at the Hamburg *Rathaus* when his racial disease was identified by a Nazi doctor? And if I did, were you listening? I can only hope you're on my wavelength now and your soul, like a radio wave, is somewhere up there in the ether on a journey through infinite time and space.

My bar mitzvah portion dealt with nothing less than the creation of the universe and, more importantly, woman, and was to be delivered in front of an audience I didn't know from Adam. The rabbi, a man with hooded eyes and pale, creviced skin, said the Bible explained, as God first created light, that the earth went round the sun. "Okay," I said, wanting to bolt from the rabbi's library and explore the neighbourhood.

On the day of my bar mitzvah, a boy in the front row of the synagogue stuck out his tongue. I chanted that God had spoken the world into being. My breaking voice made a mess of the tune. The oldies groaned after each line and my father wept. When I'd practiced swinging my new prayer shawl over my shoulders, he'd said, "Another one lost to mysticism and unreason." He'd insisted that the religious were, "Hypocrites and beggars," and I'd worried that I'd embarrass him. Yet, tears were rolling down his face. My father, the atheist, Zionist, socialist: crying in a synagogue. I turned back to the text that I was supposed to be following with my ivory hand-pointer and realised I'd lost my place.

At the time, I didn't dispute my father's godlessness, any more than I disagreed with his conviction that Schubert was superior to other Viennese composers. "And I include Bruckner, Mahler, Süssmayr, Haydn, Mozart, the Strausses, Schoenberg, Schmelzer *and* Beethoven." I didn't care. Not about God and not about Beethoven. They were irrelevant. I was into Hendrix, Dylan, and The Churchills.

The rabbi prodded my back, and I raised my voice: "This one, at last, is bone of my bones, and flesh of my flesh. This one shall be called..." I squeaked out "Woman," to sniggers from the congregation. I was paraded down the aisle, the scrolls held over my head. Sweets were thrown and I took a gobstopper in the eye. With my other eye, I saw an old woman in the upstairs gallery cheering as if she was proud of the shot. My father said, "Don't cry, boy. You did a good job."

"Blondie," a voice said.

A scramble of people tried to touch the hem of my prayer shawl as I looked for the owner of the voice. In the drizzle outside, my mother and grandparents were waiting with an umbrella. "You've done us proud," my mother said.

"Father was crying," I said.

"I know," she said. "See how important it was to him?"

"You look like Fred Astaire," my grandmother said.

"Mother," my mother said.

"Frederick Austerlitz," my grandfather said, bending to adjust my tie. "His father was a Jew from Linz. Do you remember Linz?" he said, turning to my grandmother. She raised a grey eyebrow. "Beautiful village," he said, brushing my shoulders. "Where Hitler and Eichmann went to school."

"I tell you, he's going *meshugenner*," my grandmother said.

"Just remembering things. Wittgenstein was born there. Klimt painted Wittgenstein's sister on her wedding day. No treasure to behold. That's why he covered her in gold. Kepler observed the stars from the church and worked out that we're the centre of nothing."

"Oh, be quiet," my grandmother said.

A crowd of strangers had gathered behind me. I led them from the synagogue to our house, through the mid-morning gloom. My mother had got a research job at Haifa University. I pushed open the front door. At the far end of the living room, the crescent bay filled the window. The congregants made appreciative noises. A hairy man asked my mother, "How much did this cost?"

My mother said, "Have we met?"

He said, "Mr Schwartz." He added up the room with nods

15

and glances. "This is my daughter, Shani."[3]

I looked at her, she had milk skin and dark hair, and past her at the people barging in. There was no sign of the boy who'd stuck out his tongue.

Shani said, "I saw you at school."

My grandfather pranced over with a bottle. "Hold this." He poured a spoonful. "The French know what to do with apples." He winked. I took a sip and it grazed my throat. "Now, you're a man." he said. I waited for a burp. It popped, hot and apple-flavoured. "Drink for life, *guter Junge*. Drink for life."

"And this is Dr Marzipan," my mother said.

"All right," I said.

The sun pitched up and my father told me to join him in the garden. Houses hung onto the steep slope and crumbled into the antique quarter where a wheat factory made pigeons fat. My father perused the view, with his back to the guests. They were devouring carrot salad off paper plates. The chicken fat smoked and spat and the pigeons rounded up in the air for a go at the grain silos. I felt dizzy from my grandfather's apple drink, as a large black cloud floated overhead and cracked in two. The coals hissed, and some chicken was rescued. A rainbow reached down to the white cliffs. The guests left after eating the few skewered thighs cooked through. Shani Schwartz said, "Thank you."

I helped my mother bin the paper plates. "That was a success," she said.

"Rain wasn't forecast," my father said.

"It was a blessing," my mother said. "Got them out of here." She turned to me. "You're going to be a big hit. That Shani girl liked you."

"You were impressive today," my father said.

16

"Yes, you were," my mother agreed. They discussed the need for a stone water feature to establish the garden's proportions, and I thought about Shani's dark eyelashes that were, in retrospect, not an inch on yours.

On Saturday mornings, my father's patients trudged through the living room where I slouched in pyjamas. They disappeared into a back room. Young men in leather jackets, girls drifting through, distant and unattainable and dreamlike. At school, I decided to look moody and sloped about the skipping ropes by a railing near the canteen. Shani came up to me and said, "What's bothering you? Want to meet after class?" Forgetting to drop the act, I continued to scowl and she backed away.

My mother had given me a new radio for my bar mitzvah, small and compact and American. By '68, radios were no longer cool. However, the sound TVs made was terrible and the programmes unwatchable. My radio could still take me from my room, past the golden dome of the Bahai Temple, to sweltering Mississippi or onto a boat wheeling down the Missouri. I swallowed my pride and decided to consult my mother. "Do you like any girl at school in particular?" she responded.

Shani was the only girl who talked to me, but I admitted, "I like all of them."

"In which case, how can you expect one to like you back? Sit up straight," she said.

"I like dark girls." My mother pulled back my shoulders. "Get off," I said.

"No girl is going to want a *schlumper* like you. White or black."

I left to go spying. So far, I'd caught the sagging breasts of a woman who was about my mother's age. I skulked along alleys between houses and apartment blocks. I tried to surf down a slide in the park, but my shoes stuck. I slid on my bum and wandered past a bench where a boy, brown curls falling about his face, was smoking. "Blondie," he said.

"I knew it was you," I said.

"What? Stop staring, you homo. Sit down. I've something I want to show you." I sat, and he punched my shoulder. "Want one?" he asked, holding out a foil packet. I took a cheroot, filled my mouth with smoke and coughed. "Good, aren't they?" I nodded. "Where you live anyway?" I pointed to my house. "What. That one? With the fountain?" I nodded again. He made this sound, "Pssssssssssshh." I took another suck on the cheroot and smoke rose. He put his hand out and I felt butterflies in my stomach. He sucked his cheroot and blew in my face, and I coughed, and we shook hands. His grip relaxed. I didn't want to let go. "What's your name?" he said.

"Israel," I said.

"Shalom."

"Shalom," I said.

"Shalom," he corrected me.

"Shalom, Shalom."[4]

"Let go of my hand." He shuffled a pack of cards and asked me to pick one. "Turn it over, remember it and put it back in." I picked out the Queen of Clubs, a pornographic picture of a woman with red lips and black hair that looked like you. "Good, isn't she?"

"You didn't guess the card I picked," I said.

"That's not the point of the game," he said, snatching it off me. "I've got to get going. Old man's in a mood for a fight."

18

"All right," I said. "Can I keep it?"

"Sure." He jumped up and disappeared into the park. I kissed the card and stuffed it in my pocket.

The next day, Shalom had a black eye. "Fight with the old man," he explained.

"Looks painful," I said.

"You should see him. We like to box. He used to be an amateur in Morocco."

"An amateur?"

"Had to give up because of his hands. He's a tailor. Should see him thread a needle. Like this." He snapped his fingers. "You didn't blink." He stared at me. "What does your father do?"

"Psychologist."

"He was crying at your bar mitzvah."

"What were you doing there?"

"I like to see what you milk bottles are up to."

Climbing on my bike, he told me to sit on the seat behind him. We fell onto the road. On the second try, the slope carried us to a corner where we almost pitched headlong into a car, but Shalom threaded us down the side of Mount Carmel, finally stopping by a kiosk. He cupped his hand over his mouth and said, "You're going to have to distract him. Ask how much something costs. I'll nick the mag. Meet me out here."

I went to the counter and picked up gum. "How much?"

"Twenty agorot," the man behind the counter said.

I took out a lira note to buy time. "And this?" I said, pointing to a chocolate ball covered in coconut shavings.

"Twenty agorot."

"Let's get out of here," Shalom whispered in my ear and pulled me outside.

"What happened?" I asked.

"Too high." I suddenly noticed how short Shalom was. "You've got to get it. Top shelf by the entrance. Stuff it under your top."

"What's it called?" I asked.

"*This World*," he said. Back in the kiosk, I heard Shalom asking, "How much is chewing gum?"

"Twenty agorot." *This World* didn't look especially interesting, but I reached up and grabbed it and stuffed it under my top. Shalom crashed through the door. I ran out after him. He swerved the bike into the oncoming traffic. A car skidded onto the pavement. Going faster, we reached a wall by the grain silo, where hundreds of pigeons began flapping their wings and one came straight towards me, its beak at my eye. I ducked and shouted, "What are you doing?"

We came to a standstill and he lit a cheroot. "We're fine. No problem. Now let's look at this mag."

"You could have killed someone," I said.

"They could have killed us," he said. "Show me the mag."

I gave it to him, and he smoothed the front cover and flicked through to a photo of a woman with her shirt open. On the facing page, a review of a book called *Israel Without Zionists*. "Look at her. Don't be too nice. They hate nice. Even the snob girls at your school. And try to blink every now and then."

In my father's therapy room, I found books on repressed memory that made no sense, and nowhere an explanation of what girls wanted. I decided to ask Shani. "There's a bench I like to sit on near my house. At sunset. By the Bahai Temple. I want to ask you something."

"Great," Shani said.

We met on the bench. Her hair was tied in a bunch and I tugged it. "Stop it," she said. "What did you want to ask me?"

"What do you want?" I said.

"What do you mean?"

"You know."

"No, I don't," she said.

"What do you want from me to…you know, let me kiss you?"

"Close your eyes," she said.

"I love you," I said when my lips were free.

That night in bed, I listened to The Churchills singing on the radio: "People are saying you're playing a game. I may be a fool, but I feel just the same. I'm too much in love to hear." I had a nightmare Shani was in the schoolyard pointing out all the boys she'd kissed.

I approached school next day, groggy and worried. My first class was history with Miss Weiss. "Sit," she told us. I put my head on the desk. "You, Israel, sit up. Today we're going to learn about *Anschluss*." I yawned. "The Germans arrived in Vienna to jubilant crowds. You. Switch off the lights. You, the blinds. Yes," she said, holding up film. "Or…" She switched on the projector and behind her smiling women surrounded a soldier. "You see the Austrian women happy with the German soldier? Yes? Good. There are two sides to every story. Who was not happy? Come on. Who did the Germans despise?" She was looking at me. "Jews," she said to a silent classroom. "Here we are cleaning the streets of Vienna. Can you see?" I felt sick. "Sorry I don't have a better picture," she said, and I got up and rushed to the toilet, where I waited for the bell.

When I got to the bench after school, Shalom was smoking,

looking pleased with himself. "Kissed Shani," I told him.

He appeared to be thinking. "That's right, she was with my cousin at last year's Purim party. Probably didn't know who he was in the fancy dress. I know something that'll cheer you up. Need the bike though." We wheeled to the Arab part of town behind the port cranes. A man sharpened his fierce moustache with a couple of twitches. I thought he might slice my neck with its curved edges. Shalom said, "Not far now." We came to a grove of pine trees outside a mosque decked in green bunting.

"Can we go back?" I said.

"Leave the bike here." He shook it from my grip and put it behind a cypress. The minaret cast a pale green light, and we climbed onto a skip behind the mosque, and Shalom removed a fan from a window. "Wait a minute. She'll be coming soon. Come on, Fatima."

"How do you know her name?" I asked.

"I don't."

I saw an Arab woman with angelic cheeks framed by her hijab. There was space in the circle for one eye each. We butted heads. Slipping off her clothes and underwear, she stood tall and fat, big breasted, heavy-legged. Her thick black hair reached her hips. She washed her plump body with dainty hands that slipped into her folds, and I wanted to bury my nose in her soft corners. She looked at me and winked, and I jumped down.

"What's the matter with you?" Shalom said.

"She saw me," I said.

"Impossible," Shalom said.

"She did."

"You're crazy," he said.

"Let's get out of here," I said. "They'll kill us."

"You're imagining things."

"I'm not."

"What's got into you?"

"Please?"

"You're paranoid, Israel," he said. "Let's spy on Shani."

"Leave it out," I said.

"Come on. Why does it matter if she's kissed my cousin?"

"Leave me alone," I said and hurried off with my bike.

At home, my father was cutting beetroot. "Your parents," I said. "Were they ever made to clean streets?"

"Can you lay the table?" he said.

"Were they made to clean the streets?" My father did not reply.

The next day, I decided that I would confront Shani, and after school we made our way to the park and sat under the slide. "People are saying you're playing a game," I said.

"What are you on about, Israel?"

"People…" It had sounded cool when The Churchills sang it on the radio.

"What people?" she said. "Kiss me."

I turned my shoulder. "How many boys have you kissed?"

"Just you."

"Don't believe you." Her shoulders shook, she stood up and ran away. She avoided me at school and I didn't try to talk to her.

"Blondie!" Shalom put his arm over my shoulder.

"Finished with Shani. Don't trust her," I said.

"You don't trust anyone," Shalom said.

"I trust you," I said.

"Wouldn't do that," he said, slapping my cheek.

The next day, I drew Miss Weiss as a monkey – "The Palestinians," she was explaining – scratching her armpit, holding a banana. I might have got away with it, if I hadn't spelled it out: "Monkey Weiss." My parents were called in to discuss my behaviour. The head stated that my grades were good but that I had no friends. My parents, gauging a lack of friends as a sign of intelligence, said nothing more about it.

By Passover, Shani would stand in the same circle as me. I joked through others and, by early summer, she laughed when I admitted that I was scared of pigeons. At the end of term, during the Scouts Parade, she came up and said, "I forgive you Israel."

"I'm sorry too," I said.

"I'm moving to Jerusalem," she said.

"Why?"

"We can write to each other," she said.

"Writing?"

"Letters," she said, and the first I got from her was about a cat and church bells. I didn't write back. She described a windmill. I ripped and scattered it and the pigeons pecked a few scraps. I couldn't trust Shani. Maybe I am paranoid, but I trusted you Ori and, in the end, it turned out I shouldn't have.

Can't You Hear Me Knocking, The Rolling Stones

The train to Tel Aviv, slow and crowded with soldiers, ground down the line. I tapped my fingers on the table to the rhythm of the tracks. I'd borrowed one of my father's short-sleeved shirts: cream, beige, brown-striped and unbuttoned. Shalom was traveling backwards in a paisley shirt. I was envious of his cool pointy shoes sticking into the aisle. He picked his nose. Our hair was shoulder length.

"Gonna shave it all off?" I asked.

"Not yet." He prodded my shoulder with his picking finger. A paratrooper with a brown beret manoeuvred around the guitar that Shalom had propped by his seat. "See?" he whispered.

"Yup," I said.

"That's right." Next to Shalom, an old man had fallen asleep against the window. A woman next to me was wearing a felt hat with a bobble. I smiled at her, and she tutted.

"It's fate," Shalom said.

"What is?" I said.

"This is."

"What's this?" I said.

"This is *it*," he said and banged the table. The woman next to me clutched her bag. We laughed, and I shrugged at her. Shalom dealt cards for whist. The train creaked at the junction outside Zichron. To the left, banana palms stuffed fields dried by frames of eucalyptus, to the right, a man in a straw hat swung a net into a pool, checked the fish, and flipped them back in. The Carmel ridge melted into the plain. I won a round and Shalom snatched the cards and put them in his El Al flight bag. I breathed in as if I'd surfaced from a long dive. Stone arches undulated in the far window and the sun idled somewhere above the wheat fields, where bundles of hay were resting. The sea slapped the dunes and olive-green scrub, the wild flowers blurred and, when I looked back into the carriage, purple spots floated in my eyes, and Shalom was grinning. "Love you, bro," he said.

The sight of the power station's cooling tower marked the start of the city. We pushed our way to the door. I jumped onto the platform. "Over here," Shalom said. Number five for the beach. A bashed-up Cadillac cut in front of the bus and our driver screamed, "Son of a whore." A Beetle snuck through the gap, its brake lights smashed. We decided to get beer. The sun was giving me a headache and a pipe dripped water onto my neck.

"Shit," I said.

"Piss," Shalom said.

I gave him money, and his deep voice and stubble transformed it into a crate of Goldstar. We lugged it, one arm each, down the road between stunted pines, and I leant my head back and gritted my teeth. We crossed the road into the sea breeze and, reaching the sand, we camped under wooden shades. I lit a Rothmans, and Shalom pulled out a lukewarm beer and opened it with a lighter. I found Radio Tel Aviv and Mick Jagger sang, "Help me, baby, aint no stranger. Help me, baby, aint no stranger." The beach stretched with the sax solo and met sea folding sand, and a blue and white flag flapped and jived. The bottle was warm on my lips.

Shalom stared at me and said, "This is it." At that moment, I wished I could have held onto what I was feeling. People rolling out mats, the barking nuts-seller, the blue sky that a jet plane was hanging in, the puffy trail, a bridge over the horizon, connecting us to the world and a moment of peace.

"After the army, I want to become an air host," Shalom said. His thick brows made him look pensive, almost melancholy. "Think of the pussy."

"Can't you hear me knocking?" Jagger sang.

"Can you play it?" I asked.

"Help me, baby, aint no stranger," Jagger sang.

"Play the riff," I said.

"The lick."

"Right," I said, watching him pretend to twiddle the tuning keys. "What we got to eat?"

"Hummus, peppers, usual." I loved his mother's Moroccan food and grabbed a roasted chilli. It was fiery, but the nutty hummus and a swig of beer put out the flames on my tongue. Shalom's eyes followed two girls in shorts and he called them over.

"What do you want?" said the one with shorter hair.

"Come sit with us," Shalom said. "We got beer and cigarettes and it's your lucky day."

She took off her shorts and asked me, "What's your name?"

"Israel." I fingered the rim of my beer and remembered to ask, "Sorry. What's yours?"

"Aya," she said.

"Aya," I said. "Beautiful name. Most people don't know what it means."

"What does it mean?" she asked.

"Don't you know?"

"Of course, *I* know what it means."

"Beautiful land of Israel," I said.

She looked down at her lap, and up at me and, catching me looking where her eyes had fallen, smiled. "Can you play the guitar?" she said.

"This is my radio," I said, showing her my vintage '62.

"The guitar," she said.

I screwed my beer into the sand.

"You know something," Shalom said. "Your shirt matches the deck chairs."

Aya laughed, and I picked up the guitar. My first strum had the plectrum in the sand. Aya gave it back to me, and I took a sip of beer. My father often lamented the fact that though I loved listening to music, I was no good at playing, despite years of piano lessons from my mother. He'd a habit of saying, "Schubert died at thirty-one," indicating, presumably, that time was running out for me to become a genius. "Our family lived next door to the Schuberts for more than a hundred years," he'd said.

I strummed the chords, C, D, C, D, G, and Shalom screwed his face and growled in his heavy accent, "Yeah, you got satin shoes. Yeah, you got plastic boots. Y'all got cocaine eyes..." Aya was tapping along with painted toes, and I made the guitar loud, and Shalom sang, and I was thinking, "Yes. He's right. This is it."

After three goes round, Aya's toes stopped dancing and she looked bored. I put down the guitar and took her hand, and we ran to the warm pool before the sandbank. I splashed her with water, and she laughed, and I splashed her again. She play-hit me, our stomachs touched, and I hoped Shalom was watching. Her lips were salty and hot, her tongue shy but sweet, her arms hung around my neck as if I was sucking air from her body.

She dashed away, and I swam after her to the sandbank, where we lay kissing. The sun got behind a cloud and the wind dried our wet bodies. "Think we'd better go in," Aya said. We returned to the shades, where her friend was between Shalom's legs, resting her back on him, a towel round them both. I wrapped a towel around Aya. We lit cigarettes and smoked. Aya's wet hair looped over my shoulder, inside the towel, and water dripped down my back. The sun faded, the sea cooled, the day ended too soon. By the road, cars torching flies in the dusk with lemon-yellow lights moved behind Aya's face as she said goodbye. There were two beers left. Shalom and I finished them.

"Your one was a little *sharmuta*," he said.

"Yeah, my bro," I said.

"Why do you kiss with your eyes open?" he said.

"Do I? Want to see what's going on."

"You're so paranoid, Israel. Still, I saw you out by the sandbank."

"It was the beer... Shalom?" I asked.

"Yeah," he said.

"I'm scared of going to the army."

"Don't be. You've got nothing to worry about."

When I got home, having slept the whole train journey, exhausted from beer and sun, I found my mother and father sitting in the gloom of the living room with only a sidelight on. I shuffled down the corridor to get away from them and my father said, "Israel."

"Sorry I'm late," I said.

"Don't worry about that."

"What's happened?" I said.

"I'm afraid —" my father said, and my mother flinched.

"Your grandfather," my father continued. "You know he had trouble with his lungs. Apparently, it was putting pressure on his heart. He wouldn't have felt much. Your grandmother found him lying in the garden holding an apple to his nose. He lived a good life. He was an old man." I swallowed. "It's not like he was young, not like Schubert or anything."

A week before I joined the regiment, we buried my grandmother by his side, in the kibbutz, under a Bismarck palm. Her grave got me thinking who she'd been, and why I'd never asked her. I found questions growing like weeds in cemetery paving. Where had she gone to school? When did she leave Vienna? What had happened to her parents? My mother was grateful for my interest, but her recollections seemed incomplete, like she wasn't telling me something.

In the tree opposite, the sparrows have gathered. Our car below, a Suzuki Baleno, is pasted like a Pollock. For some reason that's cheering me up. Perhaps because I've no intention of driving anywhere. The council will have to take it away, along with my dead body. I've paid enough fines in my life for them to do me that service.

I'm writing this memoir, listening to the radio, opposite the cemetery where you're buried. The bones of important people lie close. Now you know why I was a friend of the Trumpeldor Cemetery Memorial Fund. To get us plots by the willow.[5]

I took a break from writing to go for a walk on Allenby Street, once smart and fashionable, now run-down and still fashionable. On the corner, there's a strip club and, beyond it, the Yemeni quarter, where millionaires have invested in authenticity and refurbished it. I turned towards the sea. The road at that end is shabby with grim hostels and a fountain and opens in the shape of a river delta onto the beach. The sun was hot on my neck and I was excited to catch the eyes of two Muslim girls. If only I was young and Arab. I'm an old Jew. More missed chances. I never got enough experience before I met you. Things were bound to go wrong.

"Can of Diet Coke," I said, holding one up.

"Seven," the kiosk man said.

"What?"

"Seven," he said.

"Five?"

"Can't you hear me? Se-ven," he said.

"No. My hearing isn't great," I said, and fiddled with my hearing aid.

"Six then," he said.

"Great."

"You heard that all right," he said.

"Hot day all right."

"You're burnt," he said.

I'd forgotten to put on my sun hat. "How much is this?"

"Ten," he said. I tried on the hat and gave him twenty and left without taking the change.

The walk under the cliffs is new. Not like when we cuddled on succulents. In the marina, masts waved at the sun. Bikes sped past me as I paused with my hands on the rail to admire the fading light. How many more times will I see another day? I reached the bay and the volleyball nets. I sat down under the wooden shades and pushed my hands into sand that remembered the day. The waves whispered in the dark – "This is it" – echoing, for a moment, the lost feeling of having thousands of days to come.

Somewhere, Ilanit

The year we met, the Dutch company, Philips, came up with the first hi-fi stereo cassette. I must add these bits in, because you never listened when you were alive, as if you were the partially deaf one. How did you know me without them? These facts went round and round my head. I think they might explain who I am.

The innovation of the stereo cassette by Philips could have threatened the future of radio. In the end, progress was kept in check by the conservative instinct of the people. The radio is democratic. Adverts mean we, the people, control the funds, and the music is ours. Can't be told what to like anymore. Can't be condescended to. Blues was picked up on antennae in New Orleans, transmitted up the Mississippi to Chicago, and out to a waiting world.

Karl Marx's cousin, Gerard Philips, founded the Philips company. Most of the Philips family fled to the United States, just before the Nazi occupation of the Netherlands. The Philips company protected three hundred and eighty-two Jewish lives as essential to wartime production. In '66, they shoved a cassette player into the radio. By '73, with the evil of hi-fi personal stereos on the horizon, and a future world where people would be plugged into themselves, I completed basic training and got posted to the Golan Heights, in a base not far from the Druze town of Majdal Shams, where Shalom and I could indulge our passion for spicy food.

The song that was playlisted everywhere at the time was the nauseating 'Somewhere', sung by Ilanit, the Israeli entry to the Eurovision Song Contest. The song (cloying, meaningless) could have been sung by Shirley Bassey, except it's in Hebrew. You always used to say I take pop music too seriously. Like everything else, right? It was supposed to be, you said, "just a bit of fun." I'm still not sure what you meant. The lyrics had an airy blitheness – "There I saw a rainbow in the clouds. There the morning rose in white" – that provoked my growing sense of fear.

You were humming the song and picking paper clips out of a presentation, your head tilted towards your hands. Behind you, a glass vase of snow-white tulips. You looked fed-up picking at those clips, and I felt my heart drop into my belly and thump to get out and run over to you, for your gentle fingers to play with. You raised a sharp eyebrow that disappeared behind your black fringe.

"I came to get the ordnance list," I said. You opened a drawer and pulled out a ring binder. I almost dropped it when your finger touched the back of my hand. Pressing the folder to my side, I managed to say, "Thank you…"

"Officer."

"It says Liora on your desk," I said.

"You don't have permission to call me Liora."

"Officer Liora?" I said.

"Don't push your luck. There's a training exercise next week. They're keeping it quiet. Like something's on. What's your name?"

"Israel," I said.

"Israel? I'll *really* make you suffer." Your face lit up. Mine felt hot.

"Can I call you Ori?" I said.

"You can call me whatever you like if you get the hell out of here."

I saluted, and my heart sped upwards into my throat and I gulped. The air outside was cool, and I sighed and scavenged a bent stub of yours from the ground and bought a pack of Dubek – *the refreshing cigarette* – in Majdal Shams.

"You smoking menthol like a girl?" Shalom asked.

"No," I said.

"What do you want them for?"

"A girl," I said. I held a mug of mint tea to my chin and let the steam wet my nostrils. I imagined you blowing warm, mint-smoke into my face. "You know the girl in the logistics room," I said.

"Which one?" he said.

His scalp was shiny and tanned. I'd already taken to wearing a sun hat. "The one with the dark hair."

"Obviously," he said.

"Will you promise me something?"

"Wait a second," he said, fanning out his cards. He exhaled and repositioned them. "What?"

"Will you promise me?" I said.

"Not again."

"This time I mean it," I said.

"Stop being paranoid, Israel."

"I know something's up. She said as much."

"What did she say?"

"There's a training exercise. Like there's something on," I said.

"Paranoid."

"I want to take her for an ice cream before I miss the chance."

"You're crazy."

"Full house," I said, laying down my cards.

Marconi fitted *Titanic* with a wireless transmitter. Overwhelmed by messages of joy like, "See you in New York" and "Cannot wait to be with you", the signal went down. Noticing the backlog of messages waiting to be received at Cape Cod, a passing vessel, *Carpathia*, driven by commercial concern, tapped out the Morse code directive reminding *Titanic* to get on with transmission. The response *Carpathia* got was, "We've struck a berg. Save us." Marconi himself, pioneer and Nobel prizewinner, initially became a scapegoat because of the fifteen hundred dead. However, it was understood later that radio had saved lives. Western governments responded by separating the commercial function of radio from the monitoring of maritime transport. Later, radio would be used both offensively in U-boats and by the surface fleet to detect them. It always takes a tragedy, often war, for great inventions to find their ultimate expression. It's the same when it comes to love.

The next morning, I found you and said, "Here you go. Bought you a pack."

"Is that a bribe? I'll put you in jail. Where you from?" The cigarette wiggled in your mouth.

"Haifa," I said. "Sort of. The Galilee. My parents are Viennese."

"Via-what?" You came close to me. You blew smoke in my eyes and put your cigarette in my mouth, and I watched your buttocks in khaki rocking away. I didn't manage to get you on your own again that week. Shalom and I had three daily patrols, including a night-time reconnaissance round, staring into darkness through binoculars. Only the radio waves were definitely out there, and they kept bringing us Ilanit.

On the Day of Atonement, I was filling a petrol canister when you raced out of a control bunker, clipping your shirt together. After you, a man with a hanging gut, double-starred epaulettes and bald head, turned both ways to see he was not being watched, and trotted off. The base was otherwise quiet. I smoked the pack of Dubek that you hadn't let me give you. Picturing you with the colonel, I tried to settle back down. Another puff. I methodically ate two storage packs of Lotus biscuits. It was a flat morning, the clouds lethargic, as if they were in sombre mood, barely moving, as if weak from the fast I was ignoring.

Shalom said, "You're eating twice as much as you usually do."

"I'm nervous," I said.

"If you feel nervous, fast. And then you'll have the appetite to take that girl for an ice cream," he said. He put his arms behind his head and looked at the roof of our tent. "How's it going with Liora?"

"How do you know her name?" I said, thankful I had my own name for you.

"I checked it out," he said.

"How?"

"I think you've got a problem, Blondie," he said.

"What?" The stress of the conversation had me sandwiching two biscuits together and cracking them with my front teeth.

"You know who she looks like?" he said.

"No."

37

"Take away the long hair, the piercings and the tight little body..."

"Who?" I said.

He moved slowly, unfolded his arms, pushed himself up, and walked with his shoulders hunched around my chair. He came in front of me, and put his face close to mine. I had to flick between his eyes. "Look," he said.

"At what?"

"Look," he said.

"You're too close."

"Open your eyes." He fluttered his lashes.

"What am I looking at?"

He took my cigarette, sucked, blew in my face and said, "Do you remember when I waited for you on the bench?"

"Sure," I said, and contemplated his face.

"Said you're a homo, didn't I? Now, I may be no *psychologist*," he mulched the word with contempt. "But I think you're even more of a homo now than I thought you were then. I mean, she looks like she could be my sister."

"She does look like you," I said, grinning.

"Exactly like me," he said and locked my head in his arm.

"You better make sure nothing happens to her," I said. "I'll only have you in reserve."

"She seems to like you. God knows why. Your blonde hair," he said.

"Really?"

"She said so."

"I think I might be falling in love with her."

"Grow up," he said, and rubbed his shiny head.

I took the Queen of Clubs and hid it in my uniform for luck.

I felt that if I held onto it I'd have a chance with you. We went on patrol down to the bottom of the base by the barbed wire. I peered through binoculars at bending wheat. The radio was buzzing, and I switched it off and heard nothing but shuffling wind.

"I need to fix the radio," I said. "Keep an eye out."

"What for?"

"I've got a bad feeling."

"Paranoid."

"Need to change frequency. Find out what's going on out there."

"This is it. Nothing's going on," he said.

I bent down and pulled the receiver from its socket and the next thing I heard deafened me. The radio was hot in my hands. My eyes vibrated, and I struck the side of my head, hoping to get reception. I tasted metal on my lips, the light on the radio flickered and then, nothing.

Chameleon, Herbie Hancock

"Shalom?"

"Israel?"

I recognised your voice. "But Shalom…"

"Israel?"

"Sha…"

"Israel, can you hear me?"

Your voice was hazy, far away, and I was too tired to give an answer. It was pitch-black in my head, a cosy darkness, somewhere to rest. I heard jazz music. As a jazz lover, you understand what Hancock was doing, right? 'Chameleon' gave the blues to jazz fans and jazz to blues fans, and binding them together made something fresh. They call it funk. He uses the hi-hats like snares – and that bass. That bass. Such a swaggering, grinning, pimp-rolling bass. Try not to smile, try not to grow out your Afro, try not to two-step in your bell-bottom jeans, try not to wake up in a hospital bed to Hancock, syncopating, clashing, and refreshing everything with his cool.

"Israel? Can you hear me?" I tried to wave to show I could, but my arm was dead, so I wriggled my toes. "He's responding…" your husky voice confirmed.

"I hope there's no nerve damage," my father's voice said.

"Damage?" I thought. "Listen to the music, can't you father?

41

Always going on about Schubert, just listen to this. The sax is going wild. Shut your eyes, like me, and enjoy it. Stop fussing about my nerves, I'm good in here, I can feel the rhythm."

"He's got rhythm," you said, and I wondered at our telepathy.

"He has?" my father said.

"Look at his foot," you said.

"Turn up the radio," he said.

"Yes!" I thought. "Turn it up." My father had told me that he'd attempted to influence me, like this, by playing classical music when I was in the womb. Especially Schubert's Quintet in C. That's a good tune, but it isn't Herbie Hancock.

"Look, he's smiling," you said.

"I can't believe he likes this noise," my father said.

"Why criticise now?" I thought.

"Going to find a doctor," my father said.

"Go out," I thought. "Leave me alone. Happy in here. What doctor?"

I felt breath on my face tainted by the mint and baked tarmac of Dubek – *the refreshing cigarette*. I opened my eyes and blinked a few times, blinded by you looking straight at me. "Ori," I said.

"Israel." You were close to my face, but your words sounded muffled.

"I can't hear very well," I said.

"Israel. You're awake."

"What?"

"You got hit by a shell." Your eyes fell to my chest.

"Shell?"

"There's a war on. You were hit by one of the first bombs."

I considered it and said, "Where's Shalom? He was telling me how you could be his sister." A wheat field came to mind, but I felt I'd dreamt it.

"You were brave," you said. I didn't know what you were talking about, but liked the idea of being brave, especially as your eyes rose to meet mine, like two shiny balloons. "Ori," I said.

"Yes," you said.

"Don't go," I said.

You squeezed my hand and said, "Your father told me how you'd always be hiding your radio and listening to it and taking it out when you thought no one was about. That's why he put it on your bedside table. You were tapping your foot."

"You're beautiful," I said.

"Thank you."

"Beautiful," I said, and you lowered your head, and your strawberry lips, moist and warm, touched mine.

The editor of *The New Grove History of Jazz*, Barry Kernfeld, writes: "Hancock, Herbie [Herbert Jeffrey] (*b* Chicago, 12 April 1940). Pianist and composer, he was born into a musical family and began studying the piano at the age of seven, and four years later performed the first movement of a Mozart concerto…" Make sure it's the one-volume edition, published by St. Martin's Press, New York. We don't want crossed wires, mixed signals.

Clearly Kernfeld had the same classical prejudices as my father. "The album *Headhunters* (1973) marked the beginning of a commitment to more commercial types of music, particularly rock, funk, and disco and contained the hit single *Chameleon*." Well, Ori, if you want my opinion, and by now you're used to getting it, because you can't ignore me or tell me to shut up anymore, 'Chameleon's' a masterpiece *because* it's more commercial, *because* it attempted to fuse together different genres of music writing. It was popular *because* it was a fine composition. 'Chameleon' was not a man changing his musical colours. The song is not a disguise. I woke up in hospital likewise. The same Israel Shine, but a chameleon stuck the colour I'd always been inside: a deep blue.

Today, I'm writing with a funk inflection. Oh, yeah. What a happy, sad, old man I've become. I've already done a few loops around the kitchen table with the song on my computer. I'm foot tapping. I'm flicking that hi-hat, I'm grooving that bass.

"Boy?"

I'd thought my father was going to fall to his knees as he put his hand out on the curtain post. His stubble was grey around his chin, his skin yellow. I'd never seen him go unshaved. "Yes?" I said.

"Boy," he said.

"Where's Mother?"

"My boy," he said.

"Mother?"

"It's a miracle," he said. For the first time since my bar mitzvah, his scepticism had visibly cracked.

"He can't seem to hear on that side," you said.

"Just the right ear?" my father said.

"Heard that bass all right. Thanks for putting it on."

"No problem," he said.

"Where's Mother?"

"She had to go back home."

"Right."

"Yup," he said.

"Coffee?" you suggested, as if the miracle of my rebirth was running out of steam and needed pepping up.

"Water," I said.

"I'll have a coffee," my father said and started cleaning under my fingernails. I summoned the energy to wiggle my fingers. He left me behind the curtains and came back with water. He lifted my head and tipped some into my mouth.

"Good boy," my father said. "You were too young."

"Where's Shalom?" I said.

"Far too young. Even Schubert got to thirty-one."

My father said this with a frown on his forehead confused by a smile on his lips. His eyelids were red from tears. He stroked my hair, and I closed my eyes and said, "Where are we?"

"Afula," he said.

"Where I was born," I said.

"Back to the beginning," he said. "Down the corridor. In a room exactly like this. I'm going to find a doctor. They're overwhelmed."

"What about Shalom?" I said.

"I'm afraid…" he said, and I recognised the same reticence he'd used when my grandfather had died. He rubbed around my heart and I started shaking, the scar on my arm coming to life like it was on fire. With the other hand, he wiped tears from my face and said, "Let me put on some music."

"Where's Shalom?" I managed through the pain.

"They found you unconscious," he said.

"I bent down to fix the radio."

"Shhh," my father said, rubbing circles on my chest.

*

45

The scar on my forearm was pink and jagged. My upper thigh had been ripped open, but the bandages were hidden from view by the hospital gown. Still, the wound throbbed and ached, but the morphine helped.

"How are you feeling?" my mother asked.

"Fine."

"Fine?" she said.

"That's how I'm feeling."

"Fine?" she said.

"Is that a question?"

"No," she said.

"Fine," I said.

"How's your hearing?"

"Fine," I said.

"What do you remember? You should talk about it."

"Nothing," I said. "Not much. The radio wasn't working. Nothing."

She frowned. "Israel, pretending everything's all right is dangerous."

"Save me the psychology. I'm telling you, I'm fine," I said.

"Israel?"

"Leave me alone."

"Do you remember dragging Shalom?"

"Nothing," I said. "You know what I'd like? A bowl of strawberries."

"Strawberries?" she said. "You don't like strawberries."

"I want strawberries," I said. "How do you know what I like? I'm not a little boy."

"I'll bring some," she said.

On her next visit to the hospital, she brought a Tupperware box. I waited for her to go before opening it. I didn't want to be watched. I popped the green helmet off a juicy one and looked it squarely in the face. "I'm sorry, Shalom," I said, and bit and sucked and thought how well the taste would go with menthol from one of your cigarettes. I was alive because I'd ducked to fix the radio. That made sense.

You brought me Herbie Hancock's record 'Chameleon'. We listened together on father's mini-gramophone. At least I did. You filed your nails. The second song, 'Watermelon Man', had me in stitches. I told you why – a watermelon is like a chameleon, red and green. I know what you're thinking, I go on and on about the radio, I mean it did save my life, but when it comes down to it, recordings are useful. Can't sit around waiting for the radio to play the track you want.

Sure, but the point is, how would we have heard Herbie in the first place? And before that, would honky-tonk blues have crawled out from the brothels of the Deep South to infect the world without radio transmission? No. We'd still be listening to orchestras reinterpreting Bach. But the radio gave us freedom. No radio? Well, there'd be no blues, no pop, and no funk.

We first made love in the hospital. Less than a week after my re-awakening, you climbed onto the bed and, moving the sheet and my nightie aside, sunk me inside you. Your eyelashes fluttered on my neck. After, your hot cheek on mine, your thick hair covered my face, and I didn't mind that it was hard to breathe.

I'd insisted to my mother that it was luck I'd been badly injured in that initial fire. "It's not lucky," she said. She had one streak of white in the curly brown. Her features were neat, her thoughts and manners and clothes (a caramel dress with a white belt and white heels), and her house, that I wouldn't be returning to, always tidy.

"Lucky," I said. "Do you think Ori would have chosen me otherwise?"

"Liora's a nice girl," she said.

"Ori."

"Very nice. Dark."

"My light."[6]

"Very dark," my mother said, her moisturised brow bundled tight.

You parked on the kerb by the gates to the cemetery. It was raining and the paving was slick and shiny. I limped up the filthy stairs and on the second floor you opened the door. If I could have seen myself sitting here now, writing about my life in my underpants – old, fat, tired, guilty and waiting to go to the cemetery over the road where you're buried – I might have asked you to close it again. If any of us could see ourselves at the end, we'd push back. We do it every day, closing the door on our imaginations. However, as the door opened, with hope in the fresh, wet air, I turned to you and said, "Now I feel I'm home." You took me to bed and undressed me.

Not long after that, I applied to the university to study electrical engineering. I'd thought I'd enjoy understanding how the inside of a radio worked. I discovered that talk of gates and amperes explained the insides of a radio, but not what was *inside* a radio. A shift to media communications had an obverse drawback. It was too theoretical, not practical enough. After a conversation with my father, in which he clattered his teaspoon around an espresso, I plumped for a major in psychology. The spoon stopped circling, his head jerked up, a smile welcomed me to the family trade.

I'd never understood much of what I'd read in my father's library but had, by inheritance or osmosis, absorbed the rudiments of theory, and my unusual sensitivity to my environment meant I was good at reading people. In short, I'm trying to find a modest way of saying it, I excelled. There was only one person I couldn't read. You. Perhaps because you were so straightforward I couldn't imagine you were hiding something. I, on the other hand, was about to really let myself go.

Give Me Tranquillity, Igal Hod

I'd felt it was time for a new sound and it must have come because others wanted it too. Airtime was given to music that had been bottled up in underground clubs since the late fifties. The new, more honest sound, was Middle Eastern. I shouldn't have expected you to like it just because your parents were from Iraq. But the fact you hated it was incredible. I still don't think I've got over that. You shivered at the modulations, trilling and sentimentality.

You once laughed when I apologised to someone for bumping into me. With Shalom, I'd some courage, a confected swagger, but I was back to shyness and holding onto my radio, scared, apprehensive, grateful for my second chance, mothered along by your strength of character, kindness, patience and genuine indifference to what other people thought. I found it funny when you checked the details of a bill for coffee for the length of time it took to drink it.

We sat opposite the TV, squashed on the narrow sofa, our viewing taste inversely proportional to the amount of spice on our plates. You liked thrillers and cop shows like *Kojak*. I preferred *Happy Days*. On my lap, a tray of *shawarma* with chilli, whereas you'd go for salads and pizza, although you dipped the crust in my hummus. When we compromised by sharing chicken,

I lathered it with *zhoug*. I made myself lamb kebabs with pine nuts, parsley, mint and chillies from the pot I'd planted on the railing, and you boiled pasta. Your mother made chicken soup, as if your family had come from the Pale, and I'd shake pepper sauce into it. I wanted everything spicy. In the same way, I loved oriental music.

It chimed with the hot, dusty city despite its pretence of being European. The glamorous Bauhaus blocks built to the design of German modernists had already crumbled in the sea air. Their white facades matted with dust, their paint cracking in the heat. The glittering affectation of northern European architectural sensibility lost to the relentless summer sun and winter downpours.

In the mirror, I was showing signs of cracking too. My blonde hair had grown back from its military crew cut with a widow's peak, making me feel that my hair had been thickest the moment the Syrian soldiers packed the cannon and drew back the charge. My shedding hair wafted in the breeze. That's when I began to collect baseball caps. You got irritated, as if collecting them was to annoy you. I gave my reasons. You said my vanity embarrassed you. Do you remember my first, I found on a bench, a sweat-stained khaki souvenir from the Israel Nature Reserves? You hated that hat, and claimed the sweat marks were the remnants of dog piss. Despite my thinning hair, I felt energetic. The *darbuka* beats on the radio drove the blood around my body. You said, "Switch it off."

"Why?"

"Because," as if I was a child.

I'd bought a compact Sony radio with a battery life that meant I could carry it around for days. At the beach, I didn't have to worry that sand would jam it up because the speakers were blow-clean freckles in the plastic. The sound, turned up high, suited the tinny recording quality of the oriental music that you were begging me to switch off – "Please."

"No," I said and, instead of arguing, went for a walk. That is when I discovered Trumpeldor Cemetery. Such a quiet place and sad, the way the dead were trying to matter with the size and placement of their gravestones.

My parents found the Middle Eastern sound upsetting. But you? Didn't you come with your dark hair and big eyes to save me from my inheritance? Those Viennese habits, Viennese tastes, Viennese ideas that music had to be written down, crafted, structured. You agreed the new music was noise. What about letting your spirit free? Take a chance on the moment. Ducking to fix the radio saved my life. Still, at least you all got on at my expense.

It wasn't only the music. In conversations with my mother about psychology, I found myself aping my grandmother: "That's not why I want to be a psychologist. You can't know what makes us tick. We're not watches. You can't open our heads and play with cogs. We're made of mush. And even if you understand the gears, how does that help you feel the passing time? We exist in an invisible medium that makes us perceive everything else as being there. Like the radio. We are the spark-gap. Life, like music, rushes through us." I believed that nothing could be known and that everything was about spontaneity, timing, rhythm, and beat.

My mother viewed the brain as systematically as my father viewed a Schubert sonata. Psychology was, to both, a way of calculating human weakness rather than accepting the mystery of experience. Studying psychology had a strange effect on me. Much like astronauts affirming their religious faith while walking on the moon, psychology reconfirmed my view of the mystical, empty heart of our being. I didn't find learning about human behaviour changed my belief that we were unknowable.

My tutor was into Festinger, May and Kinsey. I liked Freud, despite what they tried to drum into me. That's one of the reasons I'm typing away. Freud hit the sweet spot between the theoretical and the practical. My life, as I write it, is Freudian. I started this memoir with what I saw through the dusty window aged seven. *Mizrachi* songs[7], like the one rattling from my Sony radio, had a melancholy and self-pity that suited my rehabilitation. Electric violas sound like violins trying to have a good time. Good pop tells you where you are and when. It explains what we're feeling, together, right now. Most of the time, lust and hate and love and desire, sounding subtly different every decade, but the basic components of human experience are always the same.

Children associate heat with noise and cool with silence. Tel Aviv's a hot and noisy place. The hooting, revving trucks, the breathless streets, people piled together, all with stories about where they came from. As a child, I'd dismantled my transistor radio, to try to understand where all the noise was coming from. My fingers fumbling the screws, I popped open the panel. I expected an enormous world inside. I stared at nodes and colourful wires and soldered valves. In the middle, the secret bottled in a glass tube, a vacuum, the nothing at the centre of everything.

A radio station, like a city, has its own character. We pick what to hear and we listen as one. It was no surprise the music had become hotter and noisier. I couldn't have been happier with my life, in the few years of peace, with you, after the war. It's a cliché worth repeating: you saved me. But I think we knew it couldn't last and that was another reason we were so happy while it did.

My first step to understanding what the radio meant was to treat it not as a mechanical object, but as a case for treatment. I began to work out patterns of behaviour. For instance, would a soprano vocal precede a toothpaste ad? It proved more unpredictable than that. In the end, I abandoned the material to study the medium. What was the radio? It was a lot more than wires in a box, although to understand why it was a revolution that has never stopped, the nuts and bolts must be considered. However, for my second degree, I shifted to cultural studies, and did a wider analysis of the type of programming peculiar to each country. Did you know in Japan they have a silent transmission in the afternoon interrupted by the ping of a triangle on the half-minute?

My parents argued relentlessly that the "peripatetic" nature of my studies was "unedifying." They wanted me to settle down, find a career, and have you have my child. Every time I announced that I was heading in a new academic direction, they would look at me like I was lost. "I'm fine," I insisted, but didn't blame them for worrying because, with Shalom gone, I wasn't sure what I was alive for.

I'd experienced something that should have disoriented me. But the only thing I could link to that moment of horror was my new-found love of strawberries, my wispy hair, and your love. You weren't compensation for Shalom's death but, then again, you were my only compensation. We became a couple as if you'd chosen me when I was unconscious in hospital. Although you looked like him, you didn't remind me of him because, in many ways, you'd replaced him. Our small apartment overlooking Trumpeldor Cemetery was where we developed our need for one another. I loved being stuck in the same space as you, rubbing up against you, arguing. Each time you passed close enough, I kissed you. I'm surprised you didn't push me away. I could be seriously needy.

At the time, everyone was wearing colourful fabrics, denims, long hair. Not you – black leggings and a black vest with your black hair straightened into a bob and your lips bright scarlet. I never got bored of touching your body or thinking about it. The city should have been in mourning, and it was mourning its dead, but there was an atmosphere of relief. We'd managed to find a life raft to shore. However, the sands were shifting, the sea is not far below our feet, something was making the world uncertain again.

We decided to have a baby without talking about it. When we didn't talk we were most in synch. Your eyes always lost their shine when I went on about the radio. But when we decided to make a life without a word they lit up. We tried, but nothing happened, and we enjoyed it and didn't think too much about it. I finished my second degree and was about to begin my doctorate, and you were working as a kindergarten teacher. One day, you said the children made you want a child bad and that it was getting to you. Your face when you checked the toilet paper in your hand each month, to find the clockwork spot, was painful to watch. I began to suspect those scarlet-brown stains were down to me.

My nightmares started when the peace talks began. I was often forced to leave Shalom's body, his bloody face begging me not to go, as dogs circled and barked. When I woke in the middle of the night, wrapped in sweat, I found a new dread that Freud would have called existential anxiety. I plugged earphones into the speakers of my radio and listened to late night call-ins, where everyone seemed to be stressed out. You were understanding, and I washed the sheets every few days. When I thought I was going to suffocate, I tried to wake you by stroking your back. Hearing you mumble in your sleep was enough to calm me. A sensation returned that was not a memory but something I'd experienced. I couldn't breathe. The airlessness of an explosive nothing. You started hiding your disappointment at your menstruation. "Don't hide things from me," I said.

"I'm not hiding anything," you said.

"What's wrong with me?" I said. "Why can't I get you pregnant?"

"It'll happen."

Around my birthday in '77, Anwar Sadat came to Jerusalem. "Stop shouting at the TV, it's not going to change anything," you said.

I leaned into the TV with my finger pointing at his head. "One bullet," I said. "If only I had a gun. I'd make strawberry jam of his head."

"Stop it," you said.

"Remember our holiday in the Sinai? The blue water, the crayfish, the red rocks. We made love in those waters. Son of a whore."

"I want you to go for a sperm test."

"Not now."

"My doctor says we both need to get checked out."

"Big step," I said.

"No, it isn't."

"If I killed him," I said.

"What are you doing?"

I blew on the end of my finger. "Let's go out," I said.

"Put on the air conditioning."

"I can't breathe with air conditioning," I said.

"Since when?"

We went to Pub Lick.[8] The logo was a tongue licking froth off a mug of beer. The place was packed, and the smell of spilled beer and cigarette smoke made breathing no easier. I found a hair in my Goldstar. We agreed that Tel Aviv was our romantic getaway and that there was no need to leave the city. By my third, you told me to slow down, when someone pushed into me. I was hunched, hand curled about my pint. Another push, and my chin hit the glass.

I wonder why it got to me, your not being able to get pregnant, the peace talks, the amount of beer, the hair in my first glass, but it did. I can remember the feeling of having had enough. "You want to watch this shit. Then watch it. But don't bother me," I said.

"Sorry about him," you said. I didn't like you apologising for me.

"If you want to watch the news, fine, but don't disturb me," I said. The TV in the corner had a flickering image of the Egyptian president. I imagined that's why the man was so insistently leaning on me, to get a look at the big story of the day.

"Israel," you whispered.

He leant on my back. I wriggled free and stood up. I removed his glasses and snapped them. "What the fuck are you doing?" he said. I punched him. His nose gave way. He fell, and I kicked him in the stomach. Suddenly there were hands all over me and I felt my legs dangling and red and blue lights. I leaned forwards to explain myself as we drove off.

"I fought in that war," I said.

"Sure thing."

In the police station, I gave up my wallet and keys and

signed a few documents, wanting to be co-operative. "Sign here. Sign that," a policeman said.

"He deserved it," I said.

I was led down a narrow, bright corridor, like a hospital without nurses. I found myself sitting on a mat in a cell, the door locked, wondering how I'd got there. "I fought in that war," I shouted. There was silence. I approached the metal door, and pressed my ear to it. I slapped it, demanded they let me out and asked where you were. "I fought in that war. Listen to me."

My arm was dead, and birdsong fluttered through the bars. I rolled onto my back and flicked my fingers to relieve the pins and needles. My hand was swollen, blood-stained. I stared at the ceiling and felt happy alone, locked-up, with the birds chirping. Nothing to do except think about what had got me there, in reverse order, searching the crowd of memories: Sadat in Jerusalem, a possible case of infertility, Shalom's face when I beat him at cards. I rolled to my side. I needed a radio. Anything to distract me from the images in my head. I imagined holding my new Sony in my hands, checking the frequency. I wanted to hear where I'd got to. The birds were answering the electric riffs. I sang with them, "Give me tranquillity, give me life..."

Solitude was an answer to everyone. Shalom had been killed, his death caused by peaceniks like that man at the bar. Shalom had warned me about them. The noise of opinion can be deafening. Don't let it drown out the music. He needed a broken nose to remind him of the bloody facts. Violence is a great communication tool. Words have no impact. The door opened, and there you were. "It's nice in here. No one bothers you," I said.

You raised your eyebrows and your parted lips seemed to

want to ask a question but instead you turned, and I got up and followed. I signed out at the front desk feeling hard done by, like I'd spent the night at a bad hotel and, standing at the entrance, raised my face to the sun. "Well, that was exciting," I said, trying to cheer you up.

A car hooted at the zebra crossing and I gave it the finger. You grabbed my arm and said, "No."

The pavement was sticky from figs the birds were pecking. "Where do the bats go in the day? And the birds at night?" Wherever they were, the bats couldn't be heard shrieking. "Give me tranquillity…"

"Stop singing," you said.

"Let me live…"

"Stop it, Israel."

I tried to turn you in the street, but you refused to cooperate. "Say thank you," I said.

"You're not yourself."

"I'll sing you a song."

"You're not yourself," you repeated, and we got in the car.

"What's wrong?" I said.

"It's only bail. You're probably going to prison," you said.

"We'll see," I said, not really minding the idea.

"What am I going to do?" you said.

"Start the engine. Look in the side mirror. Put it in first. Release the clutch, indicate and…" I pressed the horn. A gull staggered off a bench.

"I'm scared of you, Israel. You were so violent," you said.

"You betrayed me," I said.

You stopped the car and looked at me as if I was sick. "What did you say?"

"I'm scared."

You exhaled and rejoined the traffic and said, "You're scared? You smashed his face in. You could have killed him."

"So what?" I said. "He deserved it."

"You beat his head into the ground."

"Did I? Don't remember that. No," I said, but to be fair on your version of events, my T-shirt was covered in blood. "He deserved it. Right? I'm all right, Ori. Don't worry. Right as summer rain. There'll be more coming this winter. They love getting their heads wet."

"Stop talking nonsense. You're scaring me. Did you sleep?"

"Very well," I said. "Each summer, there's a second round of strawberries from the Golan. The high altitude allows for that later crop. Shalom made sure that we get strawberries twice a year. That's got to be worth something, right? Strawberries, in the middle of summer."

"It's something," you said.

"I need to get my things," I said.

"Where are you going?" you said.

"I never went to see his grave. Outside my parents' is that bench overlooking the bay. How many times has the sun set since we smoked those cheroots he liked?"

"I'm not sure…"

"I don't think I can have children, Ori, I don't think I *can*," I said.

"You need a rest."

"I love you, Ori. Let me sing you a song," I said.

"Please. No. Let's be quiet together."

"Why don't you like *Mizrachi* music?" I said.

"It upsets me."

"Why?" I said.

"It reminds me of the past. The past upsets me. You get dragged into it and it doesn't let go."

"I don't see how you can't like Igal Hod," I said.

"Because your family didn't come from the same place as mine. Would you listen to a German marching tune?"

"Austrian," I said.

"Same difference."

"No, I wouldn't."

"Shalom's not coming back."

"I know."

I packed my clothes in a laundry sack. Occasionally, I managed to catch your eye. "So, I'll see you in a bit then," I said, clutching my things, sort of hoping you'd try to stop me so that I could insist on leaving.

"Say hi to your parents," you said.

"Right, bye," I said.

Downstairs, I crossed the road and walked into the cemetery where, as I look out the window now, you're buried. I missed you then, when you were alive, and now that I'm writing, and you're dead. Back then, it was a bright, cool morning. I sang the Igal Hod song that had got stuck in my head: "Blue skies, sunshine in the heavens, trees moving slowly, chirping birds singing their song." I found a plot behind a mimosa bush, where I put down my things. My back was aching. The mat in the police cell hadn't softened the concrete floor.

"You're a lucky lot," I said to the chattering gravestones. I say something, you say something. Game of bat and ball. Is anyone focusing on the other guy's shot? Are you watching him? Foot movements on the sand, his preparation and follow-through.

You don't know who he is. You're watching the ball, waiting for it to come back and thinking what you're going to do with it. Conversation is ball-hitting, loneliness is the price one pays for the sincerity of throwing the game.

On the other side of the mimosa, a gravestone. I lay down in the shade and played with her name, Raziella Ben Ari, made in deep grooves. Raziella wasn't sad, or anxious, or lonely. My mouth was dry. I got up and went to the shops. On the lamp post at the corner of Ben-Yehuda Street there was a flier for a massage parlour. I tore it off and put it in my pocket.

"Lovely day," I said to the man at the kiosk.

"Lovely day," he said.

"What?"

"Lovely," he said. "Can't you hear me?"

"Sort of," I said, and handed over money for the cola and went for a stroll, past carpet shops. I'd wanted one since we'd moved to the apartment on Trumpeldor Street. However, you disliked oriental rugs as much as oriental music. You said they'd make the room dusty and hot. I pointed out that the city was dusty and hot and that, like the music, it would fit the hot, dusty city. You weren't going to budge. Not you. I've never met anyone less likely of being convinced by an argument.

"Israel," I told the carpet man.

"Eliahu," he said. He'd set up shop, mending, selling, buying Persian carpets and Afghan kilim. I guessed that, like my parents peddling psychology and classical music in the Galilee, once he'd got to Palestine, he'd realised the only thing he knew were the traditions of where he'd come from.

"Show me your best carpet," I said.

"This one's at least a hundred years old," Eliahu said.

I imagined the ancient trade routes, ceramics and spices, cumin and turmeric. Eliahu blew his nose and stray snot hit the carpet. The colours were orange-blossom and opal-green, with a pearl border infested by black, Persian spiders, symmetric, repetitive, metronomic. The colours bright – vibrating, shivering in proximity, gaining new shade where they bordered.

"It's not for sale," Eliahu said.

"Why not?" I asked.

"It's just not." I put my forehead on it. "What are you doing?" he said.

"Seeing if I can sleep on it," I said.

"Please. Stand up. It was my father's," he said, touching my back. "It's precious to me." I imagined a camel train lugging carpets rolled like cheroots from Babylon to Jerusalem, the Islamic patterns picking up the dust of Nineveh. I breathed in and sneezed. "Get off it," he said, tugging my wrist. "I'm not sure we have anything for you. I'm shutting now."

I shook him off. "It's eleven o'clock."

"For lunch," he said.

"Bit early for lunch," I said. "What about this one?"

"Don't ruin it."

I gave it a stroke. "It's good quality," I said. My knuckles had bruised purple. I patted my hair. "So, how much? You know, as a matter of interest."

"Hundred dollars."

"Don't have dollars," I said, and noticed that his bowl-sized skull-cap had the secular purpose of covering a hairless crown. I thought about getting one for that reason alone.

"Are you deaf?" he said. "Hundred dollars or I'm shutting for lunch."

I went to Discount Bank on the corner of Mapu Street, where my parents sent my allowance. I picked a paper ticket and waited. I enjoyed being in line. Nothing to do but wait my turn. "Can I have one hundred dollars in shekels," I said.

"What's your account number?"

"Here's my identity card," I said.

"I can give it to you in dollars."

"Give me fifty shekels too," I said.

"That's everything in your account."

I took the cash and skipped between traffic to Eliahu's shop and bought the carpet, in dollars. Putting a toothpick in his yellow teeth, he counted the money. "Repulsive old bastard," I thought. I heaved the carpet over my shoulder and took it down an alleyway, my back aching under the weight. I was buzzed through the door to find three girls on a couch. Behind a desk, an elderly lady with a long nose and small mouth asked, "Who would you like?"

"Oh, I don't mind," I said. The girls were smiling at me.

"Who?"

"Her," I said, pointing at the youngest looking. "As you can see," I said, with my hands in the small of my spine. "I've got a bad back. I don't want to make it worse. I'm just saying, are you qualified?"

"Fifteen shekels."

I didn't have the energy to haggle and went on, "I need a massage. Really deep." The one I'd picked, in a short, white, stretched-cotton dress, well-worn and stained at the hem, had muscular thighs and would be more than capable of working out the knots in my muscles.

"Come with me," she said. There was a single bed in her

room, floral wallpaper and a shower with mildew on the sealant. I put the carpet by the door.

"Clean," she said, pointing.

"I'm clean."

"You blood there," she said.

"Got in a fight."

The shower was hot. I wiped water off the glass. She had fat toes. I came out and she dried me. I lay down on the bed, musty, smelling of sesame oil. She straddled me, and I felt her heavy thighs gripping my hips. I turned over to tell her that my lucky card was the Queen of Clubs and to ask about moving onto my shoulders, when she reached down, and I realised my naivety. "Don't worry about that," I said and got up, but when I bent over to retrieve the towel, she smacked my bottom.

"Naughty boy," she said, and laughed in my face. I left the massage parlour in a hurry, dragging my carpet with me. I stocked up on a few cans of cola and decided on an afternoon nap in the cemetery, where I hoped to find comfort from touching the worn stone over the bag of bones that was once a young woman called Raziella Ben Ari. I bunched a handful of clothes under my head. The carpet made a fine mattress.

I woke in the evening, wet and cold. I drained the can, flat and diluted with rain. I thought of you, up there in our apartment, waiting for me to come home. I looked up and let the rain soak my face. I set off for a barber's shop. There was a large chart on the wall behind the till. A small man with an impeccably tended moustache, thick as a brush, said, "What do you want?"

I sat in his chair, the Hellenic twiddles of a radio guitar encouraging a new look. I explained, "I don't want any off the sides. If you could shave down the middle."

He peered in the mirror over half-specs. "I think it would be best to cut the sides and leave the top longer. It will suit your face."

I stared at my sullen eyes, rosy cheeks and red nose, and said, "You're going to do what I tell you."

"Are you sure you want me to shave the middle of your head?"

"From here to here." I opened my thumb and forefinger like callipers.

"Are you sure?"

"Just do it," I said. He held the buzzing razor, and I chuckled at the scene I was directing in the mirror. "Come on, let's do it. Chop off my hair." He pursed his lips. The first zip made a chunk float into the air. "Yes, that's it! Keep going," I said, bouncing in the chair.

"Keep still," he said. Another buzz. The hair in the middle of my head was razed to fluff. Using a dryer, he blew blonde curls off my polyester cloak and, shaking his head, disappeared into a cupboard. I grabbed the razor and had a go, pulling from front to back. "What are you doing?" he said, returning with a broom. "Please. Please. Give me that. What are you doing? No. Please. Have you gone mad? Give me that." He snatched the razor from my hand.

"I'm sorry," I said.

The middle of my head was bald. At the sides, two curly curtains of blonde hair cupped my jaw. He was getting on my nerves and I felt like jamming scissors into his hand.

"Give me those," he said.

A blast of wind and rain, and I tugged my shirt around my neck. I needed a drink to calm me down. However, I didn't want to go to a bar. Catching sight of my hair, a couple crossed the road. I went to the kiosk and picked up ten packets of crisps and a bottle of vodka.

"You okay?" the kiosk man said.

Back under the mimosa, I made a turban out of a shirt and put on three layers. I lay down and found the wall and ranks of gravestones acting as windbreaks. The rain stopped. I opened a can, took a swig, filled it with vodka and took another swig.

Raziella said, "You'll catch cold."

"What were you like when you were alive?" I said.

"Scared," she said.

"What of?" I said.

"Dying."

"Where are you now?"

"Right here," she said.

"How can I hear you?"

"On radio waves."

"Raziella?" I said.

"Yes?" she said.

"What were you really like?" I said.

"When?"

"Say, when you were a little girl?" I said, and stroking the lettering, closed my eyes and saw Shalom, like he'd been at the beach, looking pensive when we were young and nothing mattered.

"Why did you leave me?" Shalom asked.

"It's not Israel's fault," Raziella said. "He's got a thing about the radio. Even in the middle of a war, he's got to find the right station."

"I wanted to hear the news," I said.

"We were the news," Shalom said.

"Old news," Raziella said.

"*I didn't want you to die,*" I said.

"*But you ducked,*" Shalom said, *his face like it had been the second before I remembered nothing: green eyes and a huge smile.*

"*Because of the radio,*" I said.

"*The radio saved you. But it killed me. Look at me,*" he said. *I crawled against the wall.*

"*You left him,*" Raziella said.

"*I didn't,*" I said.

"*You did,*" Shalom said, *spitting blood.* "*This is it.*" *He took the ring pull from a can. My eyes slipped and Igal Hod sang:* "*Dark skies, the moon in the heavens. Shalom. Out.*"

"Oh, God."

"No."

"What happened?"

"I found him like this," you said.

"Boy?"

Part of me thought I might be dead. I half-expected you to put mourner's pebbles on my face. "Why did you let him leave the apartment?" my mother asked.

"I thought he'd be fine," you said. "Said he was going to Haifa to see you. He seemed happy. I was worried about myself. I didn't think he'd do this."

"Do what?" I thought. I'd only bought a carpet. And apparently died, judging by their guilt. I wanted it to be their fault, but it was probably mine.

"Look at the scrapes on his wrist," my father said.

"Where?" you said.

Someone picked up my arm. "Here," he said.

"Oh, yeah," you said.

I thought, "Is that all you have for me, my light? Surely, my death deserves more distress than that? Shalom did it."

"He was always a sensitive boy," my father said. "Liked to sleep in our bed."

"That's bullshit," I thought. "At seven, I caught you having sex in the kitchen. It was only natural I wanted my mother to comfort me."

"I told you that you were taking on a problem child," my mother said.

"I know. But I love him," you said.

"No!" The word popped from my lips and my eyes opened to find faces silhouetted on grey clouds.

"Come on," my father said. He squatted and put his arms under my armpits and tried to lift.

"Get off me," I said. "I'm not a problem child."

"A madman then," my father said. "We don't have time for your games. We need to get you to hospital. You need medical attention."

The graves were quiet. The air was lazy. Everything still. I felt exhausted. "I'll get myself up," I said, but my legs were stiff.

"Take my hand," my father said. I gripped it and my resentment faded. I sat in the back of the car and you turned and smiled, your lips, without lipstick, pink and grey at the edges. You wrapped a black bandana around my wrist. We parked in an underground lot, and you and my mother helped me get to the elevator. I felt cold. My father said, "I spent a week with him at Barzilai Hospital. He was ahead of his time. How you feeling, boy?"

"Bit cold," I said.

My mother became flustered. "What's that shirt on your head?" She tugged it off and gasped, "Your beautiful blonde hair."

"That's a fine haircut," my father said.

We shuffled into a large, white room. Luckily you can't see bacteria or insanity, otherwise hospitals would be filthy places. A man in a white coat, wearing round-rimmed metal-framed spectacles, waved a hand at the seats in front of his desk. He was accompanied by the usual suspects – Jung, Gannushkin, Maslow and Kübler-Ross – but also, hallelujah, *Civilization and Its Discontents*, all stacked on his desk.

"Israel. It's nice to meet you," the doctor said.

"I…"

"Don't worry, we're all friends in here."

"I've always been a great admirer of yours," I said, and he looked at my father. No doubt the Viennese connection had got me an interview with the legend. "What a privilege," I thought. "Maybe he can write a paper about me. Or even a book."

"Have you read my work?" he asked.

"Have I read your work? I live by it."

"Well. Your father presented me your case," he said.

"Dr Oz is a fine psychiatrist," my father said.

"Psychiatrist? Is that what you're calling yourself?" I said. "Okay. But Dr Oz? No one's going to buy that."

"My name is Oz." He scribbled something on his pad, wet his finger on a stamp sponge, turned a page and smoothed it down. I worried that I had nothing significant to tell him but began with Raziella Ben-Ari and how we can talk to the dead on radio waves. He wrote intensely when I explained that Shalom had come to tell me that I'd been responsible for his death. I suggested that if time bends and radio waves can reach the ends of the universe, they can travel beyond space-time. He didn't respond, and I demanded, "What's the spark-gap?"

"What do you think it is?" he said.

"The space where God can reach us." My father shook his head and coughed. "Raziella told Shalom it wasn't my fault. That it was…"

"I can't listen to this," you said.

"Let him," Dr Oz said.

"The carpet proves that the past is a better place," I said. "Where is it?" I leapt to my feet. "We have to get it! Let's get it. So I can show you. The carpet is beautiful. Shapes, and phantoms, the colour of blood." My father pushed down on my shoulder. I sat and said, "The dead have a different story. You don't want to hear it, that's all. Put on the radio. Listen. They're talking to us."

"Israel," my mother said with the same weariness as the time I'd said a rude word at Passover.

"Is – ra – el," I said. "We all have a view. Everyone's got an opinion. But I know that I'm right. You have to leave me alone. I'm only mad, because the situation's so maddening." The scribbling stopped. I had nothing left to say.

"You see," Dr Oz said to my father, who nodded. "I told you in '56. Post-traumatic stress disorder." Who was he talking about? How could he have formulated a theory about me already? I was one, at most two years old, and he'd never met me when he'd proposed the idea for the first time. "We need to make sure he doesn't try to do himself any harm."

"I think you might be projecting your own death wish," I said. He wrote two words. I'd expected more from my insight. Dr Oz was a fortune teller and my gypsy parents believers. "My favourite card is the Queen of Clubs," I said. "Want to know why?"

"Of course," Dr Oz said.

"Because she's the love of my life. My Light. And it's impossible to read her," I said. "You always were. Even before I met you. Don't you see? I imagined you."

"Don't embarrass her," my father said.

"She isn't embarrassed."

"I am, a bit," you said, tugging a curtain of my hair. "What did you do?"

"Why are you laughing at me?"

"I'm sorry, it's just so funny," you said.

"Funny?" For some reason, Oz thought my chatter unworthy of further note-taking. You swished my forelocks and snorted. I yawned, so wide I thought my jaw might get stuck, like that photo of the monkey in my grandmother's book, *Das Tierreich*. Once my bail was over and the police had put together the paperwork for the most open-and-shut case imaginable, I'd be neatly filed away in a concrete cell. Dr Oz filled out a clump of forms. He'd reached his conclusions according to his own prior assumptions.

I had *everything* wrong with me. I was mad, tick, paranoid and delusional, tick, tick, violent, tick. I pitied Dr Oz. He was never going to solve anything. He was a monkey with a pen and some excruciatingly shallow ideas. I stood up and seizing the pen, chucked it at a painting and only then noticed the lovely colours. "Guttman?" I asked.

My father retrieved the pen and untied the bandana. "He also needs to get this seen to."

"When we've finished, take him down to emergency," Dr Oz said, and wrote my name on the top of a file in thick capitals. "Give this to the orderly. The good news is that given your son's recent behaviour and his past traumatic history, I'm going to

73

recommend that he's not fit to stand trial. He requires permanent care. I don't wish to intervene at this stage with psychiatrics. I don't believe this mania has played itself out. I will simply prescribe something to calm him down. He needs a mental health refuge."

"What a surprise," I said.

Oz hadn't finished. "He'll have a surprisingly free life, within a set of norms, routine curfews and work. No more hanging about the university. It's doing him no good. He needs regular graft." My mother and father were beaming, having waited years for affirmation. You, in contrast, smiled at me like you were sad.

"I'm sure the judge will take my advice," Dr Oz continued. "We need Israel to gain a different perspective on his past. Israel? Can you do that?"

"No," I said.

"For now, you're going to the refuge," he said. "You'll be monitored. Don't try anything stupid."

"Thank you," my father said.

A deal had been struck, and everyone found peace agreeing to put me away, and I felt fine with that. On the way out, you put your hands on my shoulder and whispered in my ear, "I knew you were insane." I can picture your clean teeth, despite the mint smoke, a string of spit stretching between your lips and eyes glassy with laughter. Your face, in my memory, is as clear as if I were looking at a photo of you that I don't have. Undimmed, you're burnt on my mind's retina by the sunshine of your smile. "You're ridiculous," you said. "But you've got away with it."

"The hostel's not far," my father said. We passed the Central Bus Station. I found myself buckling and unbuckling my seat belt.

74

"Stop that," you said and stroked a curtain of my hair. "What was that song you were singing when you came out of the police station? Give me tranquillity…" You whisper-sang the Igal Hod song I loved. I closed my eyes and put my head on your shoulder, and you patted my cheek.

The asylum was in a concrete corner block at the end of a row of shops. The corridor to the kitchen tunnelled past a room where a fat woman was lying on her bed. "Close the door!" she yelled. A young man in a white medic's coat and black trainers dunked his teabag in a glass mug.

"Shalom," he said. He had neat brown hair, green eyes and a pudgy face.

"Israel," I said. "There's a woman down there…"

"You must be Mr and Mrs Shine," he said.

"Doctor and doctor," my father said.

"And you are?" he said.

"Liora," you said.

"I'm Shlomi. You can come visit whenever you like. Here's my private number," he said.

"Can't she call me?" I said.

"Very good, Israel. I've spoken to Oz and I think you might be the patient I need. I hear you're obsessed by radios."

"Obsessed?" I said.

"Not a typical transitional object," he said.

"It's not a transitional object," I said.

"I see you did a degree in psychology at Tel Aviv University."

"It's not a transitional object," I tried again.

"I'm writing this proposition, but that's not for now," Shlomi said. "Let me show you to your room." We found it under the staircase.

"It's tiny," I said, wriggling between the door and the bed.

"It's a refuge Israel," he said. "It's the space available. Lucky we've got room at all. We had this cleared out. It was a storage room for old junk no one wanted. But you're an emergency case."

"Worse than prison," I said, looking around the bare walls.

"You're free to come and go. If you register with me," he said.

You noticed my concern and said, "It's a bit small. What's he going to wear?"

"We have gowns for the patients to sleep in. Bring a bag tomorrow."

"Ori?" I said.

"Liora?" he said.

"Ori, don't go," I said.

You said, "I'll be here first thing tomorrow."

"First thing? Wake me up?" I said.

"I'll try," you said.

"Wake you up?" he said. "Patients get up at six."

"Oh," you said. "I'll get here for breakfast then."

"Time to say goodbye," he said.

That evening, under a dim kitchen light, Shlomi asked, "Can you tell me your first memory?"

The shadow of the kettle was like a raven and, therefore, like the radio on my grandparents' shelf. "I caught my mother and father doing it in the kitchen," I said.

"Doing what?" He tapped his pen on his lips.

I'd practiced this type of psychoanalysis at university. "You know exactly what they were doing," I said. "I think my mother was speaking German."

"German? Interesting."

"Why's that interesting?" I said.

"German's always interesting. Can you remember what she was saying?"

I imagined the faint muttering that passed through the window and said, "*Ich komme, mein Gott, ich bin verdammt ko...*"

"Right. How old were you?"

"Seven."

"And you want me to believe that you can remember what she said, in German?"

"I don't care what you believe."

He drew a set of interlocking circles. "Do you think it *believable* that a seven-year-old, on seeing his parents having sex through a window, could remember the exact words, in German, that his mother croaked as she –"

"I remember them."

"Did you know German before hearing her speak it for the first time as she was having sexual intercourse with your father?"

I didn't like his tone. "My grandparents had German accents," I said.

"But in Hebrew," he said. "Anything else?"

"There was a book in German about animals."

"I'm sure there was. You imagined it," he said.

"What?"

"Your mother whimpering German," he said.

"Did I?"

"Are you sure you haven't watched any pornographic films in German?"

"Yes, I am," I said.

"Right. And when you think of your parents having sex do

you see anything else? Close your eyes. Try to associate something with it. A song, a smell, a picture."

"Arik Einstein's 'My House Facing the Golan'. White-bean broth and – where did that come from?" I said, opening my eyes.

"What?"

"The image of a woman," I said.

"Right."

"Stop saying 'right'," I said. "I see a woman's chest with *Feld-Hure* written on it. I've seen it before."

A mosquito hovered near my ear and his pen hovered over the pad. "I have a theory," he said.

"Ori?"

"No. Theory," he said. "Your hearing's bad. Might be causing confusion."[9]

"It goes in and out. Which is strange. Like I'm losing reception or something. Can I have a cup of tea?"

"Peppermint?" he said.

"Anything with caffeine in it?" I asked.

"No caffeine," he said. "I think you're quite excitable enough. My theory concerns pre-life experience. We only have one life, Israel. The way an individual sees the world is a projection of himself, but who is that? I don't believe that you're simply suffering from post-trauma. That's such an outdated diagnosis. You're suffering from something your trauma aroused. A child's ability to form memories is constructed from observation. From his surroundings, in most cases his parents, he picks up hints. Parental behaviour is based on life experience and memory. Monkey see, monkey do. The child picks up their memories with their behaviour and inherits both the acquired memories and, more vaguely, the inherited memories the parents, in turn, absorbed in their infancy. We don't start at the beginning. We're born in the middle. In other words, we can remember things that happened to us before we're born. What did Jung say?"

I decided to show him I knew my stuff. "He said the collective unconscious comprises the psychic life of our ancestors right back to the earliest beginnings."

"Don't try to be clever. Your atavism took place ten years before your birth. It's inside you. It's not just the self that determines who you are, but the super-self, the inheritance of fear. The horror, the grotesque strand of a newly-formed trauma." He was talking energetically. I gleaned the idea that I'd carried some strangeness with me into this life and it made sense. As if, being born, I'd woken from a dream that I couldn't remember, a dream that determined who I was. An explosive nothing that made it hard to breathe. Just as I'd woken from the war. I desperately wanted to uncover that dream.

Shlomi wrote my name, Israel, in the middle of the interlocking circles and said, "By the way, you're not mad. You're completely sane. Considering what happened to you before your birth and during your life, you're rational."

"Am I?"

"Yes," he said. "Inherited memory means we're alive before we're born. Your obsession with radio? Much of what we think we've read, or seen in photos and paintings, are *inherited* memories. I want to prove that these glimpses of the past, fragments of light and dark, are imaginatively remembered. We need to pin them down. Find out who you are. And then you won't be scared anymore."

"The radio," I said.

"Napkin?" I blew my nose. "Our inherited memories can be

more influential than our own," he said. "Inherited memories are impossible to manipulate. They're hard-wired. Many problems associated with memory and identity, including suppression and sublimation, are linked." He poured hot water into a cup and dropped in the teabag from his.

"The spark-gap," I said.

"What did you do when you saw your parents—" He coughed into a balled hand. "Doing, you know—"

"I ran away," I said.

"Here you go." He put the tea down, and the steam cleared my head. "Israel. There's nowhere left to run." The fizzing mosquito pricked my neck. I slapped myself and Shlomi pressed his foot on mine. "Concentrate," he said. "It's obvious we get our worldviews from our parents. But, it's much more than that." He squeezed down harder on my foot and his jaw muscles ribbed. "To explain who we are. Nature and nurture. All the contradictions determined by two indistinct polarities. Israel. They don't get it. People don't understand you. But I do." He relieved my foot and brushed his sleeve. "Freud never unlocked inherited memory, the adopted subconscious. Freud was not a psychologist. He gathered the evidence from literature, not the people he was pretending to listen to. Up until now we have completely missed out on the idea of inherited memory as an explanation for action. If you help me, I'll write a theory based on you. You'll be the first character in history able to remember himself before he was born. And then they'll say, yes, we get that. That's the only way they'll ever understand you. There's one problem."

"What's that?" I said.

"People don't like the idea that something didn't *really*

happen. But what *really* happens?" He leant back and crossed his arms. "Moral relativity is one thing, and factual relativity another. There are always competing narratives, but does that sanction the invention of facts? Do facts matter at all? Is anyone going to believe *you*, Israel, when you tell them *your* version of events? They should be asking a simple question: what are *they* doing judging *you?* But they won't. That's why they'll call you mad."

He'd lost me completely.

"You're made by the projection of inherited memory. Whether you like it or not, Israel, you're going to be the metaphor for their guilt. Our hunger for freedom is an atavistic urge to escape our parents. We rebel against them, but we cannot escape what's already inside us. We cannot escape ourselves. What you *do* is going to tell them who they *are*. The primal urge to escape inherited memory drives us mad. We're trying to split ourselves in two. We want to know why we're different. *Why* we are *who* we are. So, we cut ourselves off from who we are. That's where you come in. You're the proof," he said.

"Okay," I said.

"Do you believe I exist?"

"You're sitting opposite me," I said.

"I don't simply exist because I'm sitting opposite *you*."

"I'm tired," I said.

His eyes narrowed like he was looking through a rifle sight. "Israel. You're the chosen one, whether you like it or not. Whatever you are is what we all are. Whatever you do will be judged. Otherwise, why would you be here? You came to prove my theory."

"I need to sleep," I said, having become fully convinced that he was crazy. Or that's what I remember thinking, now, as

I write, and I realise that all the people in my life were elements of self, perceived, as they were, by me.

Shlomi patted his chest pocket as if he were looking for a pen. "It says in your file that your parents were originally from Austria. What does that mean?"

"Schubert. Butter biscuits. People cleaning the street. We were shown a slide at school."

"Anything else?" he said.

"Piled corpses. Photos. Dead bodies. Torn dresses. The radio," I said.

"The radio?" he said. "Interesting."

"Can I borrow one?"

"No radio. No television. No phone. No mirrors," he said.

"No radio?"

"No," he said.

"How am I going to get to sleep?"

"Shut your eyes. There's nothing to fear," he said. But what I'd seen in my nightmares were bodies in the dirt, snapped necks and babies torn to pieces.

Back in my room, I twisted the stiff tap with both hands, ducked my head and swilled the lukewarm, dusty-tasting water around my mouth. I spat and banged the sink. I locked the door, pulled back the fluffy acrylic bedspread and stuffed my body into the sheets. It felt good to be in a clean bed. I hadn't washed since the massage and had slept in a graveyard. Not even what you called a 'half-body', a hips-down spritz. My armpits smelled like apples. I fell asleep and woke to soft light on the dimpled wallpaper. I moved my foot and found something heavy. I thrashed inside the sheets and turned to find Shlomi at the end of the bed.

"What's going on?" I said, my throat sore, my eyes seeped

in mucus. I could hardly see him, or hear him, my ears blocked and pulsing, my nose plugged, my head aching, swirling.

"I was watching you sleep. You had no REM. That's good. Often dreams can ruin –"

"You scared the hell out of me. How did you get in here? I locked the door."

He laughed. "Someone in your condition can barely tell the difference between his memories, imagination and dreams. All of them are equally reliable. That's why I don't want you dreaming, if possible. Waking early helps."

I followed Shlomi's directions, up the stairs to the shower room. In a white-tiled cubicle, a man was soaping his ankles. I put my nightie on a hook, pumped the dispenser and washed my face and hair. The hot water woke me, and I scrubbed my armpits. In the kitchen, Shlomi was dunking his peppermint teabag. Dust filled a sunbeam, and he picked an inkblot diagram from a pile and put it in front of me. "What do you see?" he said.

I saw a butterfly, like the many I'd used for a paper at Tel Aviv University on memory and music. "That photo from yesterday," I said, and described it: the woman's arms butch and strong, like a farmer's. Underneath her black shirt, a white vest hides what appears to be a flat and muscular chest. On her skin a tattoo: *Feld-Hure*. She's incongruously wearing a wedding ring. The photo was taken when she was in good health. The ring made me wonder what her husband felt about her tattoo.

"I remember," I told Shlomi. "The book was called *House of Dolls*."

"What about this one?" he said, putting another inkblot in front of me.

"The Queen of Clubs and…"

83

"Go on," he said.

"It's the front cover of that book," I said.

"What's in the photo?"

"A woman opening a stripy gown. She's got shiny hair and wide eyes. She looks like Ori."

"Did you read it?" he said.

"I think I did." Another inkblot and a third photo floated into mind. In it, a different woman in the same pose. Chubby, dark-haired, completely naked with *Feld Hur* written inaccurately without the final e, and no camp number underneath. "I'm sick," I said.

"Take a deep breath."

"I have to read that book again," I said.

"Not now," he said.

"Why?"

"No books," he said, raising an eyebrow.

"What am I supposed to do all day?" I asked.

He gripped my forearm and shook it insistently. "Don't let it get to you." An airplane traversed the sky and entered his left ear. "Some of these memories are reflections of things that happened a long time ago. Pieces of light that should have burnt out. Some of those stars in the sky are not shining, Israel." The airplane came out of his head. "It'll be okay."

But my memory was burning bright and I started, the words passing through me, like I was the spark-gap: "Cobbles, the cobbles were brown and shiny, and big enough for young girls to mark with chalk for their hopscotch that made their skirts float. Their giggles rose like white balloons. Their feet stomped and stuck and they cried, hallelujah! The plane trees round the square hid the seats of the spinning wheel that appeared and hid again. Hide and seek in the bushes smelling of cat piss when he kissed me on the lips and I hadn't even said that he could. He'd a charming dimple on one side and a charming beauty spot on the other.

"I kissed both and felt my father might never touch me again, if he knew about this other man, and denounce me to his friends who smoked, like ten hot coals heating the living room in the cold winters that lasted too long, extinguished by summer, so that once out, I couldn't remember if it had ever been cold. And the girls outside were giggling, and I wanted to play with them, but they said that I couldn't, I wasn't like them, you see, they said, I wasn't like them, they said, although I had the exact same dress as the tall one, you see, little Marie-Antoinettes we were, but they said we weren't the same, and the sound of the wheel's music in the distance, like the ice cream van where the water was cold and the air was filled with dragonflies, and we'd eat wild strawberries that made our fingers sticky, so that, when I lay back on the picnic mat, swirling motifs that seemed to me like snakes, and the little blue box that took my father's change outside the synagogue, coins for the fund for the East, but was the East left or right at the end of the street?

"Was it up or down, since we'd learnt at school the earth was spherical and that meant something to do with the horizon, though the teacher, a spiteful woman, snapping out comments like she was biting insects from the air, I stopped listening, and looked out the window at the clouds swirling like milk in the lake, making shapes like those on the carpet where, having day dreamt, I'd lift my hand to see it covered by ants feasting on strawberry juice.

"The Ferris wheel went high and low, and we turned and

the world got small and the world got big, and I thought it was odd that it changed size, until one day, my father pulled me out of the queue because they said that we couldn't go on the ride because we weren't like them, and I felt small, and I thought my father had shrunk, like I was watching him from atop the Ferris wheel, but that it was stuck, so that, when he tugged me, I refused to go – come now – I did, thinking it unfair, but on the way home, he picked flowers from the bushes to put in my hair, something he always forbade me do, but now we laughed and he plucked them all, daisies and edelweiss, and hydrangea he ripped off and scattered, and I stood with my hands out, petals raining onto my palms, until we reached our corner, where the dimpled stone met the cobbled street and a wooden door, that led down into a dark room, that I'd never been in and suspected was the house of a grim, old man, full of dusty scientific instruments, but the man was older than I could have possibly imagined, older than the universe, with an eyeglass and a chain of screwdrivers around his neck, a torch, that shone on cogs, and hands that dwarfed them, like my father's dwarfed mine.

"He smiled, his moustache and his lips, very old, not grim, but dusty like his instruments – I do – and a large box, polished oak with porcelain buttons – German – my father's hand was damp – fine, thank you – a roll of precious notes and at home he set it on the mantelpiece it was too big for, he balanced it there, nonetheless, and twizzled the knob and words came out the box, picked from the sky, higher than the wheel, crumpled but crisp – run, God said – and we packed, and ran, we ran…"

"Israel?"

"…we ran and we sailed on the rocking sea where the oak box that my father had taken, in place of his shoes and his

86

suits and his cane and his gloves and his hats, told evil stories but played Greek music, to a place where I was allowed to play hopscotch with the other girls, under palm trees on baked mud, but I didn't want to, no more games but cards, my grandmother who I'd never see again, except in my mind playing whist and gin rummy, putting down the Queen of Clubs." I finished, "That radio was in my grandparents' house. On a mantelpiece, it fitted just right."

"We're getting somewhere. Do you believe me now?" Shlomi said. "Those are your mother's memories. But they're also yours. You've inherited them."

I have a new Roberts pocket radio that I ordered off Amazon, with a digital screen but analogue dials to change the frequency and a wheel to set it to various locations around the world, including Honolulu, Dacca, and the Azores. It's a pretty machine with a long antenna that does nothing to improve the reception. I've had to stop writing because the memory of that speech of mine has taken it out of me. In fact, the whole process of writing a memoir is going to be the death of me.

I'm listening to *Reshet Bet*, a sensible talky station mixed with folk tunes. It's decent and moral and keeps me company and I rarely get lifted from my writing because it scarcely shocks, except today, when I'm tired writing and, in its own modest way, it's got my attention with a big idea.

Lucky it's on the radio so you can hear the American-accented Hebrew of a visiting professor at the Weizmann Institute, with stuttering enthusiasm that proves the concepts too big for the easy flow of words: *No beginning, no end, no Big Bang, no Big Crunch, no Dark Matter, no Dark Energy and that, when you shrink the universe to a point, a sing-sing-sing-ularity, the laws of physics break down.*

Revisiting equations from November 1954, we can call into question the observation of the expansion of the universe from a singu-la-la-larity, which dates the age of the universe at fourteen billion years old, but by aligning quantum theory with a new understanding of quantum gravity, the universe becomes infinitely old, removing the requirement for dar-dar-dark matter and dark energy, two invisible quantities that are better jettisoned in our journey to the beginning of time, which had no beginning, of course.

I worry that associations build no patterns, memories no picture, that it's too late in the day to worry we're dying and dead. Can we ever get out of the world that we're in, a world where history is invented, and physics has turned the stars to shadows? We'll never know who we are. Why bother trying to find out? The fires of our illusions have been put out, and the darkness of reality made illusory, and blindly we're simply and meaninglessly repeating mistakes. I'm back in the cave-space of the spark-gap pointing out the few stars I can see. The universe might have had no beginning, based on equations drawn up in November '54. And I was born in the old-new land in '54, but the new-old problem won't go away. I should learn to enjoy life. It's all I've got.

The equations that prove that the universe is infinite were formulated the month I was born. In the intellectual sense, the universe is the same age as me. And when I'm dead, the age of the universe is not a problem that will exist at all. It came into being in November '54 and it will end when I've slipped a knife across my wrist.

*

88

First storm of the winter and the refuge was quiet but for the drumming of rain on the metal gate sealing my window, the salvoes of water coming in waves. Every year, since I could remember, it came as a surprise when, out of the blue, an army of black, angry clouds killed off the summer. Boom – artillery thunder – the metal gate clattered its frame. I've read somewhere that lightning has the force of the Hiroshima bomb. I wondered if Japanese people, listening to silent broadcasts, relived the after-effects of the moment infinity, packaged in an eggshell, was dropped.

The rain sped on, and you put your head into the nape of my neck and sang: "Give me tranquillity..." The soundtrack to my breakdown, it was starting to get on my nerves. Your husky voice was cute, all those Dubeks – *the refreshing cigarette* – making you sound like a little girl with a cough.

I'd described the flood of inherited memories that Shlomi had released from me, relieving me just as the rain deflated the heavy black clouds and turned the sky that illusory blue, but you said, "I see no reason for him to make you imagine those things."

"They're already inside," I said.

"They never happened to you. I'm going to talk to him," you said.

Your shoes squelched on the lino and when you reached the kitchen I heard your seething tone: "You...no...it's not... shouldn't...stop...sick... You... No... No... No..." Shlomi's intercessions came, but I couldn't make out the words, even when I blocked my dud ear, and turned my right to the door. You said, "I suppose...okay...but... I'm not sure... I...well...yes... I suppose... Yes... Yes... Yes." You laughed and a few minutes later opened my door, smiling over a piece of cake. "Look what

I brought." You snapped a bit of icing and fed it to me. "That woman down the corridor used to be a pastry chef at the Hilton Hotel. Shlomi says you're doing very well. I'm proud of you, Israel."

"Can you bring me underpants?" I said. You drew the leg holes over my toes and slipped them up my legs. I lifted my bottom, and you pulled them snug. "What made you laugh?"

"Oh, nothing. He's funny though, right?" you said.

"Crazy," I said.

"He claims you need to concentrate on doing, not thinking. He says you're impotent, *in general.*" The random emphasis did sound like him. "Too many thoughts, not enough action. He says this cold of yours is psychosomatic."

"Oh," I said.

"He says you're absurdly scared of death."

"What?" I said.

"Stops you being able to do anything."

"I don't want to die," I said.

"No one wants to die," you said.

"He told me I wasn't mad. That my responses to the horrors that have befallen me and the people that I love have rationally made me scared."

"Okay. But I want you back home. Pretend to be sane."

"I'll try," I said and, turning over, sandwiched my hands under a cheek and thought, not about anything that I can remember, just thoughts, like pattering rain.

Weeks later, I was back in the kitchen, talking with Shlomi. "You got any of those Lotus biscuits?" I said. I'd recovered from my cold and felt permanently hungry. I could have munched through a whole pack. "I suppose I was bound to be mad. I'm surprised anyone in this country is sane."

"There's certainly a high prevalence of mental disorder amongst Jews of European origin," he said.

"Well, why don't Jews from Arab countries have a problem? If you ask me they've had enough bad history."

"*Mizrachi* Jews simply don't show as many symptoms of mental frailty. That's probably why you like their music so much. Less angst. More love. The reasons are manifold, the factors not clear, but genetically speaking they don't carry the same incidence of inherited mental disorder around with them."

"Are my children going to inherit my problems?"

"All children inherit their parents' problems. We've gone through this," he said.

"Well, it's a theory," I said. "I believe it, but..."

"Ori's a well-balanced woman."

"Liora," I said.

"Why have you got a problem with me calling her Ori?" he said. "It suits her. She told me she doesn't mind."

"Liora."

"Okay, Liora. If you have children with her maybe your problems will be balanced out. Ready for work? How you feeling?" He unwrapped a Lotus biscuit, snapped it in two and gave me the smaller half. "Tel Aviv is where the mad people come to find each other and where we psychologists come to find you. It was very brave what you did."

"What did I do?"

"You tell me," he said, and leaned back, and I realised he'd opened a session.

"I remember running," I said.

"Slowly," he said, holding my knee.

"I woke up in hospital with Ori beside me. They told me I'd dragged Shalom out. Can't remember a thing."

"The report says something different. They found you unconscious on the hillside."

"I was knocked sideways by a blast," I said.

"You remember that?" he said.

"No. I remember nothing."

"Nothing at all?" he said.

"I remember the feeling of nothing."

"You must have left him," he said.

I wanted to defend myself and a new memory came from the ether – dragging Shalom from the vehicle over the burning ground. All around me explosions were smashing the earth, but I couldn't let go of him. There was a ditch I had to get to, but dragging Shalom by his hand, I felt I was wading through blood trying to get there. I let go of him. I let go of him, yes. An explosion caught me, and I went flying. "I tried to carry him with me," I said. "I couldn't leave him there. But I didn't want to die."

"I understand," Shlomi said. "You looked after yourself."

"What do you mean?"

"It's a good thing," he said.

Each night of candle-lighting for Hanukkah, the singing became more restrained as the inmates of Shlomi's refuge realised that there was nothing special taking place, no miracle for them, just another day being told they were getting better, another Hanukkah, another year, for most of them. The miracle would be for the lamp oil to finally run out and for comforting darkness to fold in, for the candles to be snuffed and for them to be told, your suffering is over.

Shlomi told me that the ankle washer's father, a baker from Budapest, had survived Bergen-Belsen in a latrine and that he'd inherited the memory, the taste and smell of it, and believed he was paddling in shit, day in, day out. "So, he washes his ankles."

Standing side by side in front of the *hanukkiah*, I asked the woman about her time as pastry chef at the Hilton Hotel. Describing pavlova, *knafe* and biscotti for the breakfast *cappucini*, she said she couldn't stand rich tourists. I asked whether she missed working there. "Do you miss getting a hard-on?" she said.

I went for another Lotus. "These are good," I said.

"Nothing like my tasty treats," she said and licked her lips slowly.

"No, I bet not," I said.

"You look hungry. When you get your appetite back, come find me."

"Sure," I said, content that I would soon be home, safe, with you.

I stood in the doorway, hoping Shlomi would finish the call. Once he was gone, I could get at the Lotus biscuits in his cupboard. Surely, he didn't count them, I thought. I'd spent a week staring at the bubble wallpaper. Locked in my bunker of a room, I slept for an hour or so, in four-hour shifts, and thought a lot about the mistakes I'd made during my life. I'd learnt in the army to let time drift over me, to wallow in the lake of it, imperceptibly flowing by. The one mistake I hadn't made was you, but I knew that you'd found me in that hospital, so I could hardly congratulate myself for anything but ducking to fix the radio and, as a result, not being killed.

"Don't be silly," Shlomi said, waving me back from the door.

"He won't mind." I could hear a voice coming out the receiver, buzzing like a fly trapped in a glass. Shlomi said, "I'm doing great, thanks. So is he. I should be, yes. Okay, I could pop over. Okay. Okay…" He put down the phone and gave me a thumbs-up with both hands.

"What?" I said.

"Looking good," he said. "You start next week."

Shlomi tapped his hand on the door above my head waiting for me to leave. I could smell his chalky deodorant. "Doing what?" I said.

"Radios," he said.

"Who were you talking to?"

"Or – Liora," he corrected himself. "She wanted to know how you're doing."

"Pop over?" I said.

"Yeah. She wanted me to bring some clean clothes for you."

"Why doesn't she come herself?" I said.

"Look, Israel. I'll be honest with you. I've seen such an improvement." He'd hardly bothered with me that week.

"Improvement?"

"Don't be angry, but I told Liora not to visit until you're settled at work."

"Stop making her laugh. I'm going home soon. I get that I was born the son of four Viennese grandparents. My mother was saved from Hitler by a timely purchase of a radio from a man who looked like God. I saw her doing it in the kitchen and possibly muttering German. I met a friend of mine called Shalom who gave me self-confidence. Because of him, I joined the Golani reconnaissance unit. I survived to find Ori by my bed. Everything emanates from the original moment that my mother escaped Europe with that radio. I got it. When can I go home?"

"It's a pretty picture. But what made her father buy it? What was he remembering?"

"If you won't let me go, give me the biscuits."

"Help yourself to as many as you like. You're on the mend," he said.

Yonatan the radio man's grey moustache was clipped a pinkie width either side of his septum. Seventy-seven was a glory year for moustaches. Think Sadat and Begin, Lynyrd Skynyrd, the hairy guys in Fleetwood Mac, Freddie Mercury, Glen Frey, Eliahu the carpet man and Oshik Levi. It was a rare fashion eclipse, when inter-generational inter-racial trends cross paths in space-time. I made Yonatan a coffee.

The fifties, at least in the West, had been decisively moustache-free. Most Israelis, at that time, slavishly followed European and American trends. A few immigrants from Arabia clung onto their moustaches, despite the prejudices that it stirred amongst the trendsetters in Tel Aviv. Stalin's moustache had cast a long shadow. When Khrushchev turned up in '64, looking like a malevolent baby, the return of facial hair was a matter of time. I was sure Yonatan, the radio spider in his electrical web, had worn a thick one since his early teens. He was authentic. He broke into my thoughts on moustaches by mentioning, "Hitler."

"Sorry, I didn't hear you. It's this ear," I said.

"I used to make money impersonating Hitler. My moustache used to be black," Yonatan said, as if that explained his choice of impersonation. "Vanity of vanities, all is vanity."[10]

"Where did you do your Hitler?" I asked.

"During the war," he said.

His body was composed of circles. His fat head was stuck on a round body with an orbiting tyre of fat, agitated tubular fingers, round cheeks, a plump O for a mouth, milky balls for eyes and snail-shell ears. He was sitting in the middle of the room behind a table on a plinth in the centre of a loose web of wires, LEDs, radio casing, bulbs, capacitors, radio tubes, hooks and handles. A dismantled radio, guts torn out, on his operating table. His hat had Yonatan and Sons written on it, the S curling back to join the Y. I was envious and thought about stealing it to add to the collection.

"You don't look much like Hitler," I said.

"The mannerisms and the moustache were enough."

"Did lots of people come?" I said.

"Lots," he said.

"Weird," I said.

"There's nothing new under the sun. Would you know what to do with this?" he said, gesturing at the mangled radio.

"What do you want me to do with it?"

"Fix it," he said, organising the parts so that they were evenly distributed around the central electrical board.

The charred, dismembered box in front of me looked dead. "Fix it?"

"There's only one thing wrong with it," he said. "You have to find out."

The problem seemed two-fold. One, there were not as many parts as I'd anticipated, and two, the parts were like clunky pieces of masonry compared to the sleek electronics I'd been used to working on at the labs at Tel Aviv University. "How old is it?" I asked. The radio was not cutting-edge in the seventies. It takes time for technology to die out. That, of course, was to misunderstand the radio. I'd no idea the radio couldn't die. I always worried it would go defunct, but that was because I valued it so highly as a tool of communion, knowing that in a city with a few radio stations so many of us were sharing the same soundtrack, jokes, news and sports updates, that I feared its demise. We were hooked together, by the machine. Others, who had no qualms overthrowing what was perfect in pursuit of complexity, believed the radio would be killed off far sooner that it was. Even I cannot believe, as I write this on a laptop that can play any music I choose, organise it, send it to my phone, that the radio's going strong.

Like all great inventions, what lay in front of me, on Yonatan's desk, was simplicity. In the sense that, the essence of its magic was the elaboration of a discovery. It was a mechanism born of nature. The radio waves had always been there, from the Big Bang on or, as we've learned recently, perhaps forever. Marconi and Hertz trapped sound in a vacuum. They miniaturised the universe and bottled it. The spark-gap. The nothing out of which everything is made, sound, traveling at the speed of light. What divine genius. That's what I was staring at, and so overwhelmed was I, partly by pity, partly by fear, that I felt pure joy as I wiped sweat off my brow. I'd the feeling something right was happening to me and said, "How did you impersonate Hitler?"

"Shut the door," he said.

I pulled the curtain over the glass and he began waving his arms about and shouting: "*Schnell, schnell im das Juden raussen. Das Juden nichts war und die Sturmer.*"

"Pigeon German," I said.

"Close enough."

"It doesn't make sense," I said.

"Did Hitler? Enjoy yourself while you're young. Let your heart lead you to enjoyment. Follow the desires and the glances of your eyes. Banish care from your mind." The biblical Hebrew inspired me.

"I almost died," I said.

"So did I, a few times," he said. "You'll get over it."

"I lost a friend on the Golan," I said.

"You'll get over him. Just think, he's got over you."

"I hope so," I said.

"Don't hold out for hope. How sweet is the light, what a delight for the eyes to behold the sun." He was theatrical, and had the charisma to make Hitler funny, and I realised that the secret that everyone's mad and no one has a clue what's going on is enough to keep one sane. "Even if a man lives many years, let him enjoy himself in all of them, remembering how many the days of darkness are going to be. The only future is nothingness."

"Radio waves will go on forever," I said.

He rounded his table and stood next to me. I patted his back and thought that I would have been happy to grow old like him. "Remember," he said. "The only good a man can have under the sun is to eat and drink and enjoy himself." Putting his hand on my back, he opened the door and pushed me into the street. "The comedy club was right there. It was popular, my bit. People were scared, you know. People laugh when they're scared, if they're scared and free. I tell you those were good days, son. I got a few girls in that crazy atmosphere. The day the Egyptians bombed the buses, I got lucky. A Romanian girl with the most exquisite behind." He shaped a woman in the air. "Think, a little Yemeni *putz* like me sitting under a voluptuous beauty from Bucharest. War makes beautiful women do crazy things.

The club was condemned afterwards, and that thing put up," he said, sucking his teeth and picking them with a nail. "I'd already finished my routine, so I wasn't fussed."

"When did you do Hitler?" I said.

"The Italians bombed us. Haifa first, but they got us here. And some German planes. I thought they were going to turn Palestine into a concentration camp, but fortunately the desert was too much for them."

I brushed my hair with my hand and blocked the sun. "I need a baseball cap," I said.

"At the time, my Hitler went down very well. People would start laughing as soon as I got on stage." He demonstrated the pantomime widening of his eyes. "The joke was a tubby Yemeni impersonating the great Aryan. And I never said I was supposed to be Hitler, just that they knew that I was pretending to be him, which was funnier than a good impersonation."

I wondered what my mother had been up to in those days, and decided she was well out of the way on the kibbutz. She must have fled again in '48 when the Syrian tanks started tearing the barricades and outer wall. Yonatan sighed, and I imagined a one-engine propeller chasing down an Egyptian Dakota, a flying David slinging itself after an Alexandrine Goliath, across the immense flat of a bright sky, hung with electricity ropes and an abutting palm, offset by the dazzling white cement of the building below.

We returned to Yonatan's web of electrics, and I said, "Let's fix this radio."

The first thing, I thought, was to put the board back together, and reached out my hand for the vacuum tube, a bulb with a metal box inside. Modern radios have transistors but if the fault was the source of the transmission, how could I get inside the glass to fix the components?

In its simplest form, the vacuum tube consists of a cathode and an anode. Apologies for the lecture, but I feel you got away with too little technical information when you were alive and, though this is not supposed to be a lesson on the history of radio, there are things you need to know. A man called Lee de Forest made the greatest advance in vacuum tube modelling, but didn't like the music we wanted to listen to. By adding a bent wire between the anode and the cathode, called the grid, and attaching the telegraph antenna to it rather than the filament, the receptor was far more sensitive. Years after he'd made it possible, he said, "Radio is the continual drivel of second-rate jazz, and sickening crooning by degenerate sax players, frequently interrupted by sales talks."

How could de Forest, a man who'd done so much, become so disillusioned with the outcome of his genius? I was approaching the fattest vacuum tube of the bunch when Yonatan said, "No." My finger floated off it, playing a game of hot and cold as I tried to find the right one. I sensed a "No" coming and dropped my finger on the capacitor.

"Always check the capacitor first," Yonatan said, and so we did, me peering over his shoulder, watching the result of the testing eye. "Especially the paper ones. Plastic ones like this are better."

"Now what?" I asked, impatient to see him bring it back to life.

"Watch me," he said. Delighted by my evident fascination with this antique radio – he had to push me back with his elbow – he plugged tubes into the electric board and took wires that seemed loose and wrapped them over the supply. There was a stutter, like flapping paper, but behind it, like a man shouting in the wind, "Give me peace. Let me live."

"I don't believe it," I said.

"Magic."

"It's that song," I said.

"One of the tubes has gone, or the connections are damaged." His fingers were as thick as the rubber end of the screwdriver he was using to tap them. One of the vacuum tubes made a hissing sound, like a pressure cooker, and I flinched, fearing an explosion.

He removed the electricity and yanked out the tube. "Down here. Be careful, it's hot. The struts are grimy. Get a piece of sandpaper and give them a rub." I did. He jimmied it back into place, removing it a couple of times to free dirt from the socket and then, plugging the radio in, tapped it, and it fizzed. That's how simple the radio was and, basically, still is.

"You have to be methodical," Yonatan said. He tapped about with the screwdriver until there was a whistle and the radio shorted. "This one's burnt out."

"Like me," I said.

"You don't seem so bad," he said.

"I'm not mad, you mean."

"You don't seem it. Not like the rest of the people they send me."

"I don't feel it. But I think I might have been."

"We've all been at some point. The last guy they sent me wandered off and I didn't try to stop him. Scary, he was." Checking the tube on a machine, he ratified what he'd decided by saying, "Correct." He opened a drawer full of glasses, picked out a tube, stuck it in and reconnected the electricity.

Igal Hod sang: "Say thank you. I'll sing you a song," and the plugs and wires and the sound of Hod singing, near the bus station, voices shouting, the endless diesel grind, made me feel rooted, as if I belonged. I was both down here with the radio and up there with the radio – the Mediterranean guitar twists rolling me over and over in the sky. It was a feeling of completeness, of rightness, of euphoric consistency with my surroundings and I started singing along, as you do when a song carries you with it, "Give me peace! Give me life!"

"You are mad," Yonatan said, chuckling.

I worked with him for the next two months. I turned my obsession into a passion and found a reason to be happy. We ate everything with *baharat*: allspice, cardamom, cassia, cloves, coriander, cumin and nutmeg. For my part, I showed him the pleasure of burnt toast with olive oil, honey and caraway seeds. We became a father-son team. When my parents came to visit, I was embarrassed by my relationship with them. I worried Yonatan would think I was a sham, a spoilt kid slumming it. Yonatan talked with them happily, commending me to my own parents as a great boy. I, cross-armed, pretended to work.

I complained to Shlomi about their visits and he said, "Your family are part of the problem, Israel. I understand you feel that, but they're also part of the solution. You can't go back on what you are, as little as they can, and for better or for worse, you have to help each other." He brought me clean clothes from our apartment. I smelt them for a hint of Dubek that you might have been smoking as you hung them to dry.

When it was time to part from Yonatan, I felt so upset I could only say, "Your baseball cap."

"What about it?"

"I like it," I said. "Who are the sons?"

"Take it," he said, and pulled it tight over my head. I rubbed the brim between my fingers and arched it with my palms.

"Thanks," I said.

"One more word of advice," he said. "Don't hate life because it's futile and the mere pursuit of wind. Enjoy it. A season is set for everything, a time for every experience under heaven. A time for being born and a time for dying. A time for planting and a time for uprooting the planted. A time for slaying and a time for healing. I had one son. He died in a car crash." He cast his glare to the light from the doorway. I wondered at the baffled peace in his expression and thought I hadn't seen Shalom's father, the might-have-been-boxer from Morocco, since we'd been posted to the Golan. I hadn't been to a single memorial and had never visited Shalom's grave. It was time to make peace with what had happened.

"I'm sorry," I said. "I shouldn't have asked. You've given me hope."

"A time for tearing down and a time for building up. A time for weeping and a time for laughing. A time for wailing and a time for dancing. A time for throwing stones and a time for gathering stones. A time for embracing and a time for shunning embraces. A time for seeking and a time for losing." I checked the different times on a rack of radio clocks. "A time for keeping and a time for discarding." His face was trance-like. Was he remembering his son along with the words? It seemed like an incantation calling on a cherished memory, but also one that was always with him. "A time for reaping and a time for sowing. A time for silence and a time for speaking. A time for loving and a time for hating. A time for war and a time for peace." He paused and pinched spittle off his lower lip. "Ah," he said. "Getting old is terrible. It's a terrible thing. Getting old. Nothing but regrets."

Shlomi hadn't brought me clean clothes from home for a week. "You've done very well, Israel. My theory needs some work, but you've helped. I don't want to see you back here. Get going."

"What, that's it?" I said.

"That's it. Truth is you could have left weeks ago," he said. "Write a journal. It will help. Write down what happens to you and what you feel about it. Try to write honestly. It'll make you feel better. The page is a reliable ear."

"I don't know how to write," I said.

"Just write."

"About myself?" I said.

"Yes. It's the thing to do. We've all got a book in us. We're all in need of a blank page," he said.

"I can't believe your advice is to make me more self-obsessed. Write about myself. How? I have trouble enough getting through the day. Take myself apart and look at the components?"

"Try your best. Just write what you feel. Keep it simple," he said.

"Simple?" I said. "Maybe I could bring in the radio?"

"How?"

"As a metaphor to explain who I am," I said. "Different frequencies, different music, different times but, despite it all, I'm a definable thing. Some people switch on the radio and listen. Just like that. Others wonder how those invisible waves were captured from the universe. Who made them? How can they be caught in the spark-gap? You can take life at face value, or ask what's inside our heads. But the truth is, what's inside is unknowable and infinite."

"Self-obsession is the future," he said.

"How can we ever know why? Best clutch onto the radio. What makes more sense than that?"

"Nothing, Israel. Nothing makes more sense," he said.

"Like jumping up and trying to touch the sky. You know it's impossible but you try. Then you learn it's not blue at all. The impossibility becomes immeasurable. It stops you even trying. But no one solved the mystery, they simply took away the pleasure of jumping and trying to grab hold of it."

"As long as we have a future to comfort us," he said.

"I never thought about it like that. Ideas," I said. "Even the worst ones are comforting, I suppose."

"Time to go home."

"This is it?"

"That's that," he said.

On the bus back to our apartment on Trumpeldor Street, anticipating your shock at finding me on the doorstep, I understood that you were my complete future and that without you I was nothing. You opened the door and clapped and hopped on the hundred-dollar carpet.

Come Back To Me My Boy, Margol

'Karma Chameleon' kept the queue at the falafel shop on the corner of King David Street tapping its feet. A band called Buggles had already predicted that video would kill the radio star and, though I dismissed it, by the middle of the decade I was getting worried. Boy George's dreadlocks, on the screen by the till, were bright as his dreams: red, gold and green. The music video had arrived, the radio was in danger, and I felt exhausted.

In the silver tip jar, I saw my bulbous face, grey from lack of sun, my blonde hair reduced to tufts. After finishing my grape juice and a pickled chilli, I dragged myself away. I meandered through the playground behind the art museum and thought about you. Having been diagnosed with polycystic ovary syndrome, although my semen, a minor player, was apparently nothing to write home about, I worried you might lose hope.

I'd looked in a medical dictionary, and it told me that the outward signs of your condition included infrequent or prolonged menstrual periods, excess hair, acne, and obesity. But, as far as I knew, your periods waxed and waned with the moon. Your hair was black and thick, your skin smooth, your wide hips ready to cradle an embryo, your tight waist and big breasts making every second defying the odds a pleasure.

I was not a man of the times (muscle men at the cinema,

daring jet raids, Dexy's 'Come on Eileen') but a PhD student with writer's block and minor issues with the quality of his seed. Sitting in the Alice Gitter music library, it didn't much matter that inflation was in triple digits. Borrowing books is cheap. However, my subject, the role of the radio during the Holocaust, was depressing the hell out of me.

The more I researched and the more I knew, the less made sense. Given Shlomi's ravings about inherited memory, it felt important to persevere. Instead of writing about myself, I was doing a doctorate but, in many ways, the topic was me. You'd watch TV and I'd fall asleep, nestled under your breast, sheets of paper on the duvet. I woke up after you'd gone to teach. I made myself coffee in a paper cup and pressed myself into the frantic crowd on the bus, trying not to spill any. The ride home was quieter. Morning expectations, unmet by the day, had a soporific effect on everyone. In my early thirties, I had wrinkles at the corners of my eyes and deep lines either side of my mouth, even though, from where I am now, writing about myself, as Shlomi wanted, I was young back then.

However, at the time, I felt the wrinkles were marking the end of something. The street lights winked knowingly at me and the newspaper crumpled down the side of the seat informed me that there was a protest that evening. Communal outrage. I didn't have the energy to get involved with that. We'd stopped going to bars. The music scene, I gleaned from chance encounters in cafés, was simple and electric, but I'd stopped listening. I was out of the loop.

The Alice Gitter music library is a good place to hide if you're feeling down. It wasn't called that then, but the ceiling's not changed. I was spending a lot of time looking at the grey concrete.[11] Eating Lotus cookies against library rules, I'd grown a belly. "At least one of us looks pregnant," you said. Withdrawing from the future, a process that is now mercifully over, I felt lonely trying to write. Sony Walkmans irritated me. I hated the way people plugged themselves in and listened to music alone, while standing right next to you, their ears rattling like snares. It seemed so selfish. I put on the radio, for old time's sake: Marvin Gaye's 'Sexual Healing'. There's pain, there's the honest cure. But it didn't help. Jackson released 'Beat It'. Never liked Michael Jackson. Three years went by.

One evening, you were preparing fish stew and Iraqi *kube* for the weekend. You'd been learning from your mother because your food was, I made clear, the only thing I looked forward to all day. You swirled the pot and listened to a current affairs programme on the radio. "You won't believe what I discovered today," I said. "You're not listening to me because of the radio. Exactly what I want to talk to you about." You turned up the volume. Someone asked someone else a question about Natan Sharansky. "Ori?"

"Yes?"

"I found out something interesting today," I said.

"Hmm." Steam looped out of the stew.

"Ori?" I said.

"Yes?"

"I don't know how to start," I said.

"Yeah," you said, moving the radio closer.

"I don't know what to say," I said. "Please listen."

"I want to hear this," you said. "Start writing already. What's stopping you?"

"I have the feeling that a blank page might be a better

reflection of what I know than filling pages with words about something that can't be explained."

"Hmm."

"Did you hear what I said?"

"Yes," you said.

"What did I say?"

"Something can't be explained," you said.

"Come on, Ori."

"I don't know. The page you're supposed to be writing on. No point telling me. I can't remember anything. That's what a page is for."

"Forgetting. That's a sign of growing old," I said.

"Not this again. You're not old, Israel."

"I feel it. Starting to really hate myself. And the way I look," I said. "Must start writing down the inherited memories."

"I thought you didn't believe that stuff."

"I don't. Not really. But it's an idea," I said. "I feel it's my duty to explain something that I can't."

"If you write something, I'll read it. But stop talking about hypothetically writing. I can't hear the radio."

Focus, or these words will blur. Look away, and I'll disappear. Today, I feel more strongly than at any time since I started writing my memoir that I'm a fake and that writing is the most mendacious thing of all. "Don't you want to know about the Sing-Sing boys?" I said.

You shook your head and said, "Not particularly. I'm trying to relax. It was parents' day today. They wind me up. They're the real babies."

"Put on some music," I said. "I need to get out of this mood."

"Tell you one thing," you said.

"Oh yeah?"

"You're too old for pop music."

"Not yet."

"Okay," you said, and thankfully, with a twist of a button, the radio played: "The dust of the streets is in his curls. God look after him. I gave him all he loved, weaved in a golden wire..."

I stood up, clicking fingers, and strutted about. "Stop it," you said. I turned you round by your shoulder. You pushed me away, your smile so wide it made your eyes water. We ditched the stew and made love – then again in the early morning with the windows open.

The theory behind my doctoral thesis was that radio is the ultimate civilising force in that it makes the prohibition of art, information and opinion almost impossible. As I discovered, the Nazi Party had agreed, and made listening to foreign radio illegal. They're always one step ahead of you in the past. I rejigged my theory to suggest that the breaking of the communal bond enabled the slaughter. That was the through-line, to be backed up by examples of clandestine jazz recordings and what they in turn said about the human capacity to endure, but the truth was the radio had played its part on both sides.

It's not that I couldn't find a lot of information supporting my initial point. It's just that I sank into uncertainty. The mounds of information only made it worse. Now one can type Sing-Sing boys into Wikipedia (I wrote most of that article). Here are my old notes: swing crosses Atlantic on radio waves. *Entartetekunst* (I can imagine my mother moaning that word as I type). 'Degenerate art'. Musically, any form of abstract expressionism, jazz, atonality, Negro or Jewish. European ghetto klezmer and black ghetto jazz, fused by the genius of Benny Goodman, a moral obscenity.

The Swing Youth – 1935 – Hamburg, Berlin and Frankfurt. The Gestapo torture; suicides common. Himmler orders seventy swing girls and boys to concentration camps. More deported to Theresienstadt, Buchenwald, Bergen-Belsen and Auschwitz. I knew what I wanted to say. The banning of radio and jazz was indicative of evil and that listening to shared music was a triumph of resistance and the human spirit. It wasn't an original thought. See Abie Nathan's fraudulent Voice of Peace, broadcast from a ship anchored off the Tel Aviv shore. Research into jazz in the camps (more on that later), and in Paris under the jackboot, made me increasingly confused.

Firstly, radio turned out to be both a force for good and evil, something I found hard to accept. How could God have created those radio waves, why would that Jewish genius Hertz have captured them, to organize the killing of His/his people? Even if my original point was valid, it was utterly futile since Radio Berlin had broadcast Wagner from Bayreuth, and honey-tongued propaganda from the mouth of Georgia Peach. And the Germans were technical innovators. In '36, the portable *Olympiakoffer* allowed folk to hear about the triumph of their race on the track. Radio helped murder millions. The use of radar, the U-boat struggle, things tangential to my original proposal that I didn't pursue too far, except as garbled endnotes, were further static. Glenn Miller had died coming back from entertaining the troops. I didn't have a clue what I was trying to say.

Fortunately, you said something for me. "I'm…"

We hugged and jumped up and down, looking at each other to picture our own relief. Your lips tasted of Dubek menthol, gone for the next nine months. I submitted my thesis at the end of June, unfussed that it wasn't up to much. I had taken it too seriously. After all, I'd started my doctorate to avoid work, and my parents, generous as always, fearful of a relapse, continued to pamper me. It ended up a sequence of vignettes, never getting to the essence of the matter, because the essence was impossible to reach. In the end, I discovered back then, there was nothing to say about anything.

As I write now, I believe I may well be repeating my mistake. A life is adefinable.[12] Time blows identity straight through us. The words, amassing themselves in delicate patterns, cancel each other out. In the beginning, the word was God. Man was made in his image. Man sinned and the word cracked into many pieces. Words don't make sense. That's why, although I keep using a song to frame the chapter headings, I can't get close to the feeling of what it was like to hear Margol singing while you cooked, or your breath in my ear when I stroked your pregnant belly.

The summer was brighter than it had been for years. The sun was like a saxophone. Traffic limped along, arms dangled out of windows, light burning skin. My hair was like straw, and my scalp red. I pulled on my baseball cap with Yonatan and Sons written on it. The sea shrivelled into itself, but I had a new sense of purpose.

"Too hot for lizards," I said, staring at the graveyard from our open window.

"There aren't any lizards in Tel Aviv," you said, patting your pregnant belly.

"Not this year," I said. "Oof. How you feeling?"

"I've never seen one here," you said. "Have some water."

"Thanks."

"I put some grapefruit in it."

"Great," I said.

"No lizards?"

"No lizards."

"Knuckles," I said. We bumped fists. You'd not been brought up in a household where kissing was normal. Perhaps I should go back and include that in the opening chapters and mention that mine was?[13] "There were lots of lizards in the cemetery," I said.

"I wouldn't know," you said. "Did you go back there?"

"No. But I'm sure there are lizards there."

"They used to wriggle and sniff in the undergrowth at home," you said. "In the pine needles."

"Yeah, they still do." I'd caught sight of one when we'd visited your parents the week before and you'd told them we weren't planning to marry despite the pregnancy. I'd decided that marriage was unnecessary. Your parents tried to guess the truth and, to protect me, you said, "It was my decision."

"There must be lizards in Tel Aviv," I said.

"Not that I've seen."

"This is nice and cold. Thank God for the icebox. If only he'd turn down the sun," I said.

"It was a good idea, the icebox."

I peered out the window, squinting through wet lashes, and considered her claim that there were no lizards in Tel Aviv. There were lots inside my head. Salamanders slithering through the keyhole into our bedroom as I slept. I can't think why they kept on coming into my dreams that way.[14] Salamanders, notoriously, are so cold that they put out fire. Maybe it was wish fulfilment and I wanted to be a salamander, so I could put out the blazing sun. "Are you sure there are no lizards in Tel Aviv?" I said.

"I haven't seen one," you said.

"Like salamanders," I said.

"Salamanders? Where did you get that from?"

"Salamanders," I said. "Chameleons too. Herbie Hancock and Boy George."

You suggested I needed to get out more, and I tried the cinema in the Dizengoff Centre. *Hannah and Her Sisters* was hilarious, particularly Woody Allen's face during the hearing test, before being told he didn't have cancer. I also liked Schwarzenegger in *Raw Deal*. The script was terrible – "This is what they must mean by poetic justice" – but Schwarzenegger's biceps were monumental, as was gunfire without blood.

I spied a girl with blonde hair in a ponytail, wearing rainbow tights and a lycra bra, in the basement of the shopping mall. She walked through glass doors to a reception. I followed and came across rows of women panting on running machines and men curling weights. I took a tour with the trainer. She was muscular, and I felt the need to state that my being out of shape was because I was 'an academic'. She looked at me like I was nothing but fat. We came to the mirrored pit where big men stared themselves down. I told her that I slept too much, had recovered from a psychotic episode and barely had the motivation to be part of anything involving other people, except at arm's length through the medium of radio, when she stopped and said, "We're all here because we want to make better versions of ourselves."

"I'm not. I want to be like him." I pointed at a tanned gorilla, hair frothing out the back of his string vest, his socks pulled to his knees. He lifted his vest to wipe sweat off his cheeks. I heaved two dumbbells off the rack.

"Sir, you're not supposed to," the trainer said.

"Watch me," I said.

"Hey," Gorilla-man said.

"He's not supposed to train without the proper shoes," the trainer said.

"Watch me," I said. At the top of the curl, I felt my bicep burn.

"Give him a chance," Gorilla-man said.

"But…" the trainer said.

"Yeah," I said, and scrambled the weights back into place.

Gorilla-man put out a hand for me to shake. He tugged my arm back and forth so hard that I missed his name. I tried, many times, to overhear someone else using it.

"Welcome," he told me when I came in wearing red and white Nike Jordan pumps. I watched him on the lat pulldown machine. His muscles screamed for air. The science of the weights room was satisfying. Time didn't matter. We were stardust pumping iron. I believed in myself. I began eating healthy. I felt alive. No biscuits or dessert, though I ate strawberries when I needed something sweet. Lots of broccoli, asparagus (I liked the way it made my pee smell) and Greek salads. You'd given up smoking and got into the diet too.

"Keep eating like this and we'll live forever," I said.

On the Lebanese border, a stone and terracotta village called Metula hangs over a valley plunged between the Golan Heights and the high ridge of the Manara cliff. The main street leads from Pioneer House, to a barbed wire fence. Beyond it, the military zone shields the border. I suggested we go, and you said, "Are you mad?"

"Not this time," I said.

"I'm seven months pregnant," you said.

"So?"

"Isn't it dangerous?"

"Don't know," I said.

"No," you said.

"It's beautiful," I said.

"No, I'm not going."

"Don't you remember looking down at it from our base on the Golan? I wanted to take you there for ice cream."

"Ice cream?" you said.

"You were busy," I said. You looked like you were thinking, but I knew you better than that. "Ori?"

"Yes," you said.

"Do you remember the man with two stars?"

"I don't like ice cream."

"I know that," I said. "I can't imagine there will be another incident in Metula. Lightning doesn't strike twice."

"It does in this country," you said.

"Come on, it'll be good for us. All we're doing is waiting for our baby. Let's enjoy the wait with a change of scene. Call it a holiday. Ori?"

"Yes?"

"So?"

"What?"

"Let's go to Metula," I said.

"It'll be freezing."

"White Christmas," I said.[15]

"What Christmas?"

"It will be great if it snows. We can cuddle up. It says we have a fire in our room." There was a guest house on the main drag I'd found with coupons from the army veterans' calendar.

"Cheaper than staying at home. Come on," I said.

"Okay," you said.

We borrowed your mother's Ford Cortina. It had a built-in radio. I fiddled with the stations, and you told me to keep my eyes on the road. I pointed out how, over the shortest distances, the frequency warped. To make my point, an Arabic call to prayer briefly interrupted 'Walk Like An Egyptian' by the Bangles. That song was my first driving-with-the-radio-on-feeling-of-elation. We fist-bumped outside Carmiel and stopped for lunch at the Sea of Galilee.

I'd planned to show you where I'd grown up and my grandmother's old house on the kibbutz, but rain intervened. I did insist, however, on stopping at the Rambam's grave in a boneyard outside Tiberias. I ran from the car with a map over my head, put a rock on his headstone and said a prayer. From the Sea of Galilee, we wound past the Church of the Miracle of the Loaves and Fish, where tour buses pumped out smog and grey-haired women with buck teeth and stooped men wearing backpacks and sandals with socks. By the Church of the Beatitudes, the sun broke the clouds and a shaft of light nailed the lush green. I put my foot to the floor, desperate to get to Metula by sunset. We rushed past Rosh Pina, guarding the Hula valley, its red roofs growing on the side of Mount Canaan like poppies.

My wet clothes and the car radiator were making the air heavy. To my right, clouds circled the dormant cones of the volcanoes, and I saw what I dreaded and loved – the Golan Heights, a high ridge blown out of the valley in great plumes of lava millions of years ago. The view of my childhood, the place I'd lost my friend. The very top of the Syrian-African rift valley, once home to dinosaurs, now basalt boulders, wheat, villages, vineyards and barracks.

"How long left?" you said, filing your nails.

"Don't you want to look at the view?"

"Not particularly," you said.

"That's where we met," I said. "You were fiddling with paper clips."

"How do you remember stuff like that?"

"Don't you?" I said.

"Only if I really try."

The road tilts up to a pine grove hiding Metula's cottages. Our room was in a wooden hut at the back of an old woman's garden. The bathroom felt like you were stepping outside, the tiles cold like the snow that hadn't fallen despite the single-figure temperature. My piss steamed, and I held my breath and swayed from foot to foot, to counteract the aching in my calves. The mirror showed my happy face. A reflection hardly shows what you're thinking. Except, my grin summed up my mood exactly. "Don't you remember the two-star colonel?" I shouted, folding my hands under the hot water, cleaning myself and making faces in the mirror: sad, terrified, exuberant, relaxed, angry.

"I don't know what you're talking about," you said.

"That guy. Week before the war. You came out buttoning your shirt," I said.

"You were spying on me?"

"Yes," I said. "Except I have no idea what went on in that bunker."

"You know," you said.

"I don't," I said.

"You can guess."

"I can guess. But I don't know."

"I can't remember."

"You can't remember?"

"I don't think so."

"Don't think so?" I was pulling the skin on my neck to straighten the wrinkles round my mouth. "Ori?"

"Yes?" you said.

"You said you don't think so," I said.

"Are you going to repeat everything I say?"

"I'll try not to. It's just I can't believe you don't remember," I said.

"I probably could remember. Can't be bothered. It doesn't matter."

"I don't know how you live like that," I said.

"Like how?"

"You forget about the past so easily." I said. "Ori?"

"Yes," you said.

"How can't you remember?"

"Should I wear a coat to dinner?"

"It's cold. Yes," I said.

"Why did you bring me to this place?"

"To buy you an ice cream," I said.

"Why?"

"To complete something I wanted to do a long time ago."

"You got me anyway," you said. "Without the ice cream."

"But I might have got you without people dying."

"It's freezing cold, and I don't like ice cream. You hoard memories. There's no need for them, because you never use them. All I remember is, I didn't like that colonel. He was rough and had a beard. You had smooth skin. I thought of you when he was kissing me."

"Did you know a war was coming?" I said.

"I pushed him away and ran outside," you said.

"Did you know about the war?"

"There were rumours."

"And you let us go out on patrol?"

"It wasn't my decision," you said.

"Is that why you came and found me? Were you feeling guilty?"

"No, Israel. I didn't feel guilty. I wanted to see you. Your fine blonde hair. You know I adore those little white flecks on your forearms. I heard you'd been hurt. I came to the hospital. I fell in love with you as you lay in bed. All that matters is that I love you. I felt like you were my child," she said. "Now, you've forced it out of me can we get going? I'm hungry."

In the mirror, there were tears reflecting myself looking back at myself. "Thanks," I said, and I couldn't help thinking that you'd played your part in Shalom's death. The fact that you'd replaced him, and looked like him, made it natural.

Golan cows are better than anything from the Negev. The only serious meat in Tel Aviv was off Ben-Yehuda, in a place for tourists, called the Whitehall Steak House. It was good, but the cuts in the Galilee came America-sized. I thought it a shame they weren't shipped to town. There'd be a feeding frenzy. The waitress gave us our menus. She had a ring through her nose. "Moo," I said.

"Really?" you said.

"Moo," I said, and ordered a 700gram T-Bone. You shook your head and I thought that you'd helped kill my best friend. I could see the top of your pregnant belly over the table. Perhaps you were going to give birth to him as restitution. At the gym, Gorilla-man had told me that to become an animal you had to eat like one. I wondered how gorillas got so big chewing sticks, but realised he meant an animal like a lion. "Nothing can be made of nothing," I said. "Something has to die for something to live."

"But it's not worth it," you said. "You're paying for a piece of bone. The bone is going to cost more than our room."

"Now we're here, I may as well go all out. This is our last time together, you and me, before our lives change forever. The last time your face will sit opposite mine and I can look in it without you being distracted by a child. Ori?"

"Yes," you said.

"I said it's the last time –"

"Can you get the waitress?" you said, and lined up the salt and pepper.

"Can't you?" I turned around to the empty restaurant. The barn, a cowboy boot nailed to the wall, was quiet except for a scratching cat. "Whoa!" I said.

"You're going to have to try harder than that."

"What do you want anyway?" I said.

"Water."

"I think I'm going to have wine," I said.

"Wine?"

"Yes, I think."

"You making a lot of money with your teaching?"

I got up and threw open the swing doors, one rearing back and hitting me. "Oo-aa," I groaned. The girl with the nose ring was staring at me from behind the counter. I remembered one trip to Kibbutz Ein Gedi when I was convinced everyone brought up there had sex in middle school. "Can we have a glass of water and a bottle of red wine," I said.

I told you a bottle of wine was on the way and your

eyebrows disappeared incredulously behind your black fringe. I was about to ask you to marry me.

"Here's your water," the waitress interrupted.

The moment passed. It took another four years to come again. The wine was from the Golan. Thanks to Shalom. The next day, I didn't have the courage to drive up there.

I woke up early and checked my Casio watch. It was six-fifteen, but I was excited. I ran a finger along your smooth back, you grumbled and, not wanting to wake you, I put on my clothes from the floor, found the room key, not without stubbing my toe on the bedstead, and slipped out, opening and shutting the door quickly, to let in as little light and cold air as possible.

The morning slapped my face pleasantly, and I felt like I'd never had a better night's sleep, cuddled up with you, your bump warming us both and making me calm. The red wine, a cabernet sauvignon, and the T-Bone, rare and lathered in chimichurri, put me out the moment my cheek hit the feather pillow. I wondered why we didn't buy feather pillows for home and remembered how expensive they were. It didn't help that you slept cheek to the mattress. You'd learnt to turn on your side as the baby got big and squashed down on your insides. That's how we'd begun to spoon for the first time in our lives, and I slept better than ever with your thick hair in my face.

I clapped my arms around my body and jogged on the spot. Between towering cypress trees, the milky valley in the dawn light. The sun was waiting over the Golan ridge, and the air was heavy with dew. I picked a pine cone from the crazy paving and chucked it. It fell short of the road. A tractor passed by and although I waved good morning the old man in the seat, jaw jutting forwards, stared straight ahead. Blue tits and sparrows whizzed and twittered between the cables that sagged between uneven masts. The cottages felt empty, as if the town had been left abandoned, for the farmer and the early birds.

The road sloped past a hotel called the Alaska Inn. Outside, a plaque commemorated the owners, a Hannah and Israel Weinberg, who had survived the Holocaust, and immigrated to Israel in '48 with their piano, no doubt hoping to play Schubert in the new country. A sparrow checked this way and that from the gable over the entrance and dived off towards the valley behind me. I continued down the slope to the barbed wire. Army jeeps, and an APC, exactly like the one I'd served in, except the radio antenna was much longer, parked in a circle around a wooden table in a yard of oak trees.

I could tell from the lettering painted on the vehicles that the soldiers posted here were from my unit. I tried to find someone to talk to. A pair of boots on the dashboard was all I found. I decided to let the soldier sleep. He'd no doubt been up all night and after sunrise, before the change of shifts, was a good time to nap. The barbed wire spliced the end of a stone bridge. Another plaque marked the action to destroy the bridge in '46 to shut off supply routes to the British army. It had been successful, it was written, but my eyes saw a venerable arch without clear signs of damage or repair. It had also been the site of the massacre the year before that had made you think twice about visiting Metula. In the thin light of a cold morning, it seemed peaceful, like a bridge from a different time, cut off by the wire that made it impassable.

Only the sound of a river running underneath made it real in the present. I remembered a walk down the Iyun Gorge as a child. My father had a romantic fascination with flowers and hedgerows. He'd pick black irises and a flower called *Darbanit* and my mother said, "Is that *Rittersporn?*" A dragonfly alighted on a leaf and water crashed in rainbows over a cliff. My mother said, "It reminds me of the *Wienerwald.*" My father collected verbena and sage to make one of his bitter, medicinal teas and, when I stung my heel on a nettle, found dock leaves. We strolled up granite steps through plants that made a tunnel and out into the sunlight that spread a golden blanket over the escarpment. Angry thistles grew by the rough, grass path and butterflies with mysterious lilac eyes on their wings fluttered like lashes. Up onto the edge of the precipice, and my father kneeled and pointed down the valley. "In the distance," he said, and I shaded my eyes with my hands. "The Sea of Galilee. Our house must be right there. On a clear day, I bet you could see it." Except he didn't say that, I remember now, he said, "I bet you could *watch* it," the feeling of a past buried in his strange vocabulary, ever so slightly wrong. And now I was going to be a father, I thought how strange my child would find me.

Now I'm writing, my parents are dead, and I've dreamt of visiting them, in the house by the Sea of Galilee, and they're in the kitchen, knocking about, unbothered that I've been neglecting them for years, and they haven't aged a day, from when I was seven and I caught them at it. We don't say very much to each other in this dream, but I'm cleaved by guilt and happiness that they're getting on fine without me, until I wake, and realize that they're gone.

Touching the barbed wire, I decided to walk around the other side of the village, back to our wooden hut, having, according to my digital watch, spent seventeen minutes out of bed. The path led around the fence and back on itself, up a steep hill. At the top of the hill there was a radar station, its bubbles and antennae searching Lebanon, plucking radio waves out of the air.

Underneath, there was a lookout point, named after the ex-chief of staff, David "Dado" Elazar – a man who might have prevented Shalom's death. His memorial post commandeered a view over the whole Lebanese frontier. It was quiet, and I took a piss at the side of the road. I tracked back and cut through lanes where flowers were tumbling from porch walls despite the cold. My hands were tingling from the icy wind, and I decided to warm myself next to you. I opened the door of the hut quickly. "Israel?"

"It's me," I whispered.

"Israel," you said.

"Go back to sleep. I'm coming in," I said, and closing the door and locking it, got into the bed next to you, and the baby inside you was like a small fire.

When I re-entered the delivery room, having left you because your screams were too much for me, you said, "Better now." Your head on a sodden pillow, your hair curly, your eyes vague from the epidural.

"One last push," I said. There were screams from between your legs, and I thought I was going to collapse, but held myself up by the rail round your bed. I couldn't look, but watched your face, tired and concerned, your chin touching your chest as you searched for your baby. Those screams were meant for you and you knew what to do, and I, being in your aura, was once again a child. Your eyes grew big and tears of sweat dripped down your temples. Our baby was screaming, and you cooed, and I remembered my mother's touch on the back of my neck. I patted the baby's back and stroked your hair. "She's perfect," I said.

"I don't…" you said.

"Perfect," I said.

"I can feel her heartbeat," you said.

"She's so hot."

"What should we call her?" I said.

You looked at the top of the hairy head, and said "Liat."[16] You nestled her inside the green hospital gown you were wearing. Head down, our baby, Liat, couldn't have been more perfect.

I stood by your side and said, "Look what you've done." I smiled at you and you picked up Liat. I wondered how I recognised her. Where had I seen that miniscule wrinkled head before, and those opaque, flecked eyes with their Asiatic lilt? She was chewing her lips, as if she was trying to feed herself. Her feet had a noticeable gap before the big toe, and her head was round as a ball, like mine. In profile, her lower jaw over-bit the upper. Her ten fingers were all there. You rocked her, bounced her and, tired, closed your eyes, and I slipped off to the doctor.

I knocked and said, "There's something wrong." I pushed open the door and, seizing on my concern, he strode past me.

"Which one?" he said.

"This one," I said, and he yanked back the curtain.

"Now, what's wrong?" he said.

You looked panicked at the sight of the doctor. "Nothing," I said to you.

"Let's have a look," the doctor said, taking the baby.

Your arms searched the air, zombie like, your frown crushing your bothering eyes. You looked at me, angrily, upset, and said, "What's happening, Israel?"

"Huh, hum," the doctor said.

Liat was crying. "Israel?" you said.

"Nothing," I said.

You gathered your baby, and Liat chewed her lip. "Can you come with me?" the doctor said. He had to pull on my elbow.

"What's wrong?" you said.

"Nothing," I said. "Just making sure all's fine. You know what a hypochondriac I am." You took Liat and peered into her tiny face. Finding everything beautiful, you laid her on your chest and the midwife fussed, apparently oblivious.

The doctor strode ahead of me, and I crab-walked behind him, eyes behind me. He pulled out a chair. I sat and wrung my clammy hands. He swept his white coat behind him and cracked his fingers. One eyebrow cocked, he cleared his throat, "Huh, hum. I'm afraid, Israel...would you like a glass of water?"

"I'm sorry?" I said.

"I'll explain," he said.

"Don't. It's my fault. I'm sorry," I said.

"What for?"

"For everything."

"This is not that abnormal in such a late pregnancy. Nor one in which there has been some trouble in conception." I shook my head. Words, circumnavigating, you understand what they're getting at. Like a jazz improv, you know the unspoken melody that's holding the phrase. I drank some water.

"I'm afraid," he said. "There are no two ways of saying this." The Hippocratic oath tells them to cut straight with a sharp knife. "Tests..." Three ways of beginning to say something. I shook my head, to mix the words going into my ears, to dilute them, make them more indistinct, because I knew what I already knew. Just like I'd recognised her. "Your daughter's suffering from a condition known as Down syndrome."

"This is it," I said.

"I want you to understand that it's not the end of the world," he said.

I laughed. "They'd have killed her anyway. May as well double down with a disability."

"What?"

"She's not suffering," I said. "She's perfect. Happy as I could ever be."

"Who is?"

"She is. And I am," I said.

"Still…"

"Suffering? Suffering doesn't smell like a newborn baby," I said.

"Mr Shine –"

"Doctor," I said. "She's alive. I'm off to see my wife and daughter. You do the tests you need, get the statistics in order. Just tell me when we can get out of here and take our baby home."

"I just want to make it clear you understand what I've told you," he said.

"Understand what exactly?" I said.

"The situation."

"I'm not sure you do," I said.

"Do what?"

"I'm not sure you understand the situation," I said.

"I would like you to know that in the worst-case scenario your daughter may not be able to walk, or even sit up."

"In the best-case scenario," I said. "We're all dead."

"I understand you're upset," he said.

"I understand. For the first time in my life, I understand. And I don't want to waste my time with you."

I powered down the corridor. You nodded at me to take Liat. "All's fine," I said. I lifted up my daughter, housed in soft cotton, and said, "Perfect. You get some sleep, then we're leaving. Never go near a hospital. They might diagnose you with something. Remember when they said I was mad? Well, I'm not."

We brought Liat home from the hospital and lay her in her cot, and I found myself singing Margol to her, even though she was asleep: "I waited all night..." Liat's skin was new and translucent. Her big toe, separated from the others, a sign of the double chromosome. I wondered how to break the news to you.

The medical dictionary: *Down's (Down) Syndrome. A genetic disorder in which the affected person usually carries an extra chromosome.* (Yes, yes, and?) *The condition is named after...*(Who writes this stuff?) *The disorder is characterised by a particular physical appearance...*(Yes, it is) *and learning difficulties, with the affected individuals having an INTELLIGENCE QUOTIENT (IQ) ranging from 30 to 80. 'Normal' is 100.* (She'll be marginally less capable than the rest of us idiots, I thought, looking at the gravestones). I shut the book. My baby girl was gurgling in her sleep, her pink tongue barging out, spittle dribbling onto her fingers which she was stuffing near her mouth.

Her eyes moved, and I sang about a bouquet of roses. My arm over the edge of her cot, I flicked a point of cotton at the side of her cover. I was in a good mood, for reasons that were, given Liat's condition, selfish. "Schubert died at thirty-one," I whispered. "Nothing clever about that. You're all mine." I pressed her button nose and wondered what she was dreaming, scrunched up under my hand.

Later that month, you said to your mother on the telephone:

"Israel doesn't have a clue. Not a clue. He keeps on picking her up and playing with her even when she has a cold. I swear he's going to kill her." To be fair, I hadn't considered the trail of mucus from her nose. "Mum. Wait. What now, Israel? What are you talking about?"

I'd put Liat back in her cot and was holding up the medical dictionary. "Cicatricial pemphigoid," I said.

"What's that?" you said.

"Something she doesn't have," I said, and held the book high and shook it. "Tell your mother that I've got a list of over a thousand diseases, ranging from the lethal to the unimaginably awful, none of which Liat has."

"He's being clever," you said, waving my arm down.

"Cicatric…tell her. Liat doesn't have it," I said.

You put your hand over the speaker and kicked me away. "I know. He thinks he's being clever. Yes, I think you're right. Still mad. Both of them. Wrong in the head."

"She's mine all right," I said.

Go Get Used To Her, Etti Ankri

"I slept with him," you said.

"What?"

"Sorry?" you said, like you hadn't heard me.

"The flower man?" I said.

"Sorry," you said.

"The flower man?" I repeated.

"Shalom." Or that's what I heard you say. I was distracted by 'White Christmas' playing from the flower man's radio. We'd stopped to pick up a bunch on the way to your parents. Your confession was weird, like a Jew writing 'White Christmas' during the Holocaust, or it playing from a radio in central Israel during a long, hot summer. Our daughter, Liat, was dribbling in the rear-view mirror.

"All right, my bro?" the flower man said.

"Some tulips. No. That pot of cyclamen," I replied.

"*Akhla*," the flower man said.

If Irving Berlin had immigrated to Palestine, I'd thought as Liat smacked the top of my bald head, he would have kept his given name, Israel (like me), and plausibly sung about a *Sukkah* stitched from *Kinneret* reeds, and other things might not have happened. But Berlin, or Baline as he was born, didn't come here and, trying to make good the past, I said, "Let's do it."

133

"Do what?" you said.

"Come on," I said.

"What?"

"Marry me."

"Really?" you said.

"Really," I said. Liat screamed, and you hugged me.

Six months later, I found myself driving to our wedding. Etti Ankri's 'Go Get Used To Her' on the radio: "Din din nah track-adoo nah nah. Din din nah. Put out everything that's burning. I'm already going crazy with someone else. What? You're going?" I loved that song. It's funny and says all that needs to be said about heartache. Only nonsense makes sense when you're that upset: "Din din nah trackadoo nah nah." I understood the quandary Ankri found herself in and, checking my side mirror, moved into the middle lane and upped my speed. I gripped the wheel tight and the weather forecast came on. I didn't want to change station because the car was shuddering like it might fall apart.

The weather in Tel Aviv can be plotted long wave from winter to summer and back again. It's a predictable arc, not a daily event. The odd storm whips up some static, but the reception is otherwise clear. It will be sunny. The one stable factor in this region. The weather forecast is, therefore, somehow more worthless than pundits predicting peace, predicting war. There's a reason civilisation was born in the Eastern Mediterranean, war being one of them, the weather being the other. The forecaster told me, as I looked around a cloudless sky, that it was expected to be, as it ought for late May, warm and settled. The engine vibrations were making my nose itch. I slowed down, switched off the radio and scratched.

The motorway cut through the towns of Holon and Bat Yam. The sea is invisible beyond the dunes where distant cranes mark the port. To the left, green mesh was protecting delicate crops and herbs from the worst of the sun, aphids and other insects. A fly had got into the car and, flustered, was buzzing about the windscreen trying to escape, occasionally looping around to hit my face. I swiped the air. Another ten minutes, driving south, and I reached the flower man I'd bought the cyclamen from, pulled over and wound down the window. The clever fly took his chance and buzzed off before I could take my revenge.

I looked in the mirror on the sun visor. I had a rim of blonde around my ears and a few sprouts on top. The earth won't stop spinning, not in our lifetimes. As it spun, I fancied the centrifugal force was taking my hair with it, a clump each equinox. I was now undoubtedly middle-aged. The sheer number of days I'd taken part in and the arrival of my daughter Liat, needing my constant help to get through the new ones given to her, seemed to slow life down. An illusion that made me content. The mania of youth replaced by gentle revolutions. Wrinkles fanned out from my eyes. I tried not to think about the fact you'd told me, right here by the flower stall, that you'd slept with Shalom. Can't begrudge a dead man that, I thought, but I did.

It reminded me, as I dithered over what flowers to buy on our wedding day, of the allegation that Shani Schwartz had secretly entertained Shalom's cousin at the Purim party before we met. But Ori, you told me, straight out, you'd slept with Shalom. Wasn't it a sort of infidelity? It was infidelity on Shalom's part and it made me think that, if he'd not been killed, he might have stolen my chance with you but that, in a strange way, you'd seen him off by not telling us a war was coming.

The flower man, with his hip pouch, bare knees and Doc Martens boots, crept up in the side mirror. "Do you remember me?" I said.

"How's it going?" he said.

"No more white Christmases," I said.

"What?"

"Israel Baline," I said.

"That your name?" he said.

"Part of it."

"Which bit?" he said.

"Israel."

"Bunch of roses, Israel?"

"So, you do remember me," I said.

"Can't say I do."

"Do you have any tulips?" I said.

"Sure do," he said. "Here you go."

Clearly my moment of suffering, trying to get money out of my pocket, you crying beside me, was not memorable to him. I put the yellow-pink flowers in the passenger seat and handed him the cash. "Wish me luck," I said.

"Good luck," he said.

"I'm getting married."

"Okay, my bro. Taking flowers to your own wedding?"

"Yeah," I said.

Would I have even proposed had I not found out about you sleeping with Shalom? It was late afternoon when I got to the village down the dirt road channelled at first between funereal cypress and then shaded by eucalyptus and oak. It reminded me of the garden outside my grandmother's house, where I'd sit with my radio, listening to Mississippi blues and ponder the apples that hung over the fence, until the stars came out. I parked behind your parents' two-storey cottage, with a porch out front, two hammocks between the posts, and a *dunam* of turf for the squirrels to run around. I hoped the rabbi would mention my grandmother.

I guessed what food your mother had arranged. Her hummus, the exaggerated cumin, garlic, lemon and the sprinkling of paprika, was enough, with the crispy bread she baked, to keep everyone happy. I said, "Come on Israel," to pep myself up and then repeated what you'd told me, "The only thing you have to do is turn up."

I peeped around the hedge and pondered the fact that it would be the third time a rabbi presided over an event in my life. The first, when my penis was clipped. Thank God, I couldn't remember that. The fourth time, and I assumed no divorces, I'd be thanking God if He turns out to exist. Liat was squatting, trying to catch a cat by its tail. People were kinder with her around. I hated the idea of performing in front of family. I emerged from the bush and was mobbed. I embraced a circle of boy-relatives with new-recruit swagger. Old men, rocking on swollen knees, slapped my back. In the distance, I saw you in your white dress, your hair rolled up. I picked up Liat and paced over. Your eyes rolled. "You look…" I said.

"I feel it," you said. "I thought I'd hate it."

"…absolutely…"

"I did my own make-up. What do you think?"

"Beautiful," I said. The exhaustion of caring for Liat, of feeding her and being patient with her, had made your almond eyes shrink and your lips dry, but you had a charm that broke through your tired face like sunshine. "Ready to become Mrs Shine, Ori, my light?"

"Hmm," you said.

"Is my mother here?" I asked.

"Abba," Liat said and put her wet hand in my mouth.

"Not yet," you said.

"Need to get her a seat," I said.

"All sorted."

"The chemo's killing her," I said.

"Not now. She'll be happy to see you marry at last."

"Mrs Ori Shine," I said.

"Liora."

"You're my reflection," I said.

"So, smile and shine my darling Israel." Despite my failings, despite being the man I was, you wanted me. Perhaps the trick was letting people down. They appreciate you more and enjoy forgiving you for what you've done to them. "Those shoes," you said.

I looked at my trainers. "I know."

"Those for me?" you said, touching a tulip.

"For your mother."

"You really are sincere."

"I try to be."

I watched the chairs being put out in rows on the patchy grass. "Israel, get over here. We need you for the photos," your mother said. I plodded over and gave her the flowers.

"What am I going to do with these?" she said, the prune-coloured bags under her eyes creamed over. We grinned self-consciously at the camera, except Liat, who had a forever-smile, unless she was screaming. The twilight spilled lilac into the yard. Moths and midges were cotton-white as fairy lights picked out their wings. The trees turned detective, their leaves hazy silhouettes. Starlings played. People were cooing at me. My mother sat, wearing her wig, on a chair in front of the canopy. My father stood by me, hand on my shoulder. Her cancer had aged him. They were both now on the last stretch, tired but stubborn. Liat was jumping up and down. The rabbi mentioned my name and you laughed and whispered, "Your shoes."

"Nike Air Jordan," I said. "Just for today."

The rabbi spoke about the mutual duty of man and woman, as two halves of the mirror image of God, to reflect the divine in their union. Your face was distant under the veil. With your hair tied up, I could admire your fragile neck and the smile on your rose-petal lips. I took the ring from the rabbi and said, "You are betrothed to me by this ring according to the laws of Moses and Israel." The crowd clapped and sang, and we waited for the rabbi to perform the seven blessings, and my mind wandered: "Din din nah trackadoo nah nah. Din din nah."

I'd disappointed everyone, the first time, when I'd plucked an apple from the branch that overhung my grandmother's fence. It was agreed that the apples belonged to the Arbel family even though in a kibbutz everything was communal. I was too young to understand the subtleties. I climbed on a crate and tore one off. Later, I learned, as if the explanation meant anything, the Arbels needed the apples for their cider vinegar. The vinegar was distributed to everyone in the kibbutz. There was a shared interest in keeping the Arbel apples for the Arbels. Sharing was something I found troubling, in any case, and the apples overhung my grandmother's garden and, most of all, I hated vinegar. My grandmother made me apologise.

"Didn't mean it," I said.

Mr Arbel ruffled my hair. I should have explained his

apple vinegar stank. Breaking the sacred kibbutz rules, he gave my grandmother an extra bottle. Over my head, the rotten consolation was passed. "Boys will be boys," he said. I didn't look up, certain I would burst into tears. I felt guilty that I'd put my grandmother in the position of taking gifts from a man. Had I not taken the apple, I wouldn't have given him the authority to humiliate us. Grandmother was pleased with me and gave me one of her butter biscuits – *Austecherle*. Hardly a *balabasta*, they reminded her of Vienna. Her memories could make her ill. She'd retire to her bedroom with a migraine. I sneaked in, to find her in the dark, with a wet towel on her forehead. Once, I feared she was dead and pulled her fingers until she groaned.

My father's parents died before I could remember them. Pictures gave me a sense that I knew them. The man in pinstripe with a side-parting from the top of his left ear, pensive, deliberative, made anxious by life. My father, with less excuse, inherited a nervous understanding of the value of art and literature. No pop music in our house. I had to discover that for myself, on the radio he bought me. He listened to Schubert on repeat. The *Lieder*, like my grandmother's *Austecherle*, relics. Smells and music and memories linger in the air. I suppose his unease with his surroundings, the breeze-block hut on the lip of an escarpment overlooking the Sea of Galilee – I imagined, when I was little, that he could reach the water with his hairy toes – was made easier by reading. The escape he could hold in his hands. I believed he would have been a happier man without the expectation he put on himself to write a seminal work on psychology, a wish unfulfilled.

My grandfather was found dead in the garden, holding one of Mr Arbel's apples to his nose, sniffing at it, and the farcical rules. I learnt it was possible to cheat and be a good man. He was caught in the act by a heart attack. Some lucky people are born with nothing to prove. My closest friend, Shalom, and my daughter, Liat, did what they pleased and made everyone happy doing it. Liat, blessed as she is with no sense of self-loathing, had a magic in that grinning head, like Shalom's. I held her hand tight. "Abba," she said.

"Yes, darling."

"Abba" she said. She had green eyes, like his, seaweed entangling you, and her expression, at rest, had the same pensive melancholy. The rabbi sang, "Pleasing Zion with her children's return" – the fifth blessing. Liat tried to loosen the bow in her hair. I let it out, and she said, "Ouch Abba," while smiling. I was impressed by the two-inch beehive I'd invented, making her round head more oblong. I knew, despite what others presumed, that she'd inherited the shape of my head, without any chromosomic interference along the way.

"My princess," I whispered and wiped crusts of mucus from her sticky nose. I kissed her head, smelling the oily, rich scalp, and patted her bottom. I looked down at my shoes. I'd forgotten to follow orders and buy myself a new pair of leather brogues for the wedding. I'd borrowed a suit from my father. He had a few because of international conferences he attended. I envied his going abroad. Flying off because people wanted to hear what he had to say in Oslo, Seville and Turin. My academic career at Tel Aviv University hadn't got me anywhere. Apparently, the radio is not as intriguing as the human mind. Unless you understand the collective psychology that forms and is expressed by it.

The conference I'd hosted at Tel Aviv University during my first semester as a junior lecturer had been an attempt to clarify my position on the radio as the ultimate expression of faith. My opening speech was intended to encourage the participants and obliquely justify further funding. "The business of academia is the flow of ideas," I'd said. "Without cross-fertilisation the forest of thought will wither." Nods from the young women in the front row, corralled to attend for better grades, and respectful glances ceilingward from my colleagues at the back, as if they needed the blank space to better arrange my words.

Not a single smile at my 'forest of thought'. It was supposed to be witty. I continued, "In the current environment, the ozone of tradition is being worn away by the toxic aerosol of relativity." I looked around. They were contemplating my words as if they meant something, CFCs being all the rage at the time. "The forest of thought must be watered with investment and new generations of students brought forth from the fertile soil to reach for the sky. Your very breathing is the ozone that protects our flourishing mental life. That is what we great chestnuts of the faculty want. For you to be receptive conkers of wisdom dropping upon the rich floor of our intellectual undergrowth. The compost of our ideas." No one was listening to me, back then, even before the internet distracted us forever.

I imagined that conferences full of psychologists were polite orgies for thinking perverts. Which is why the suit of my father's I chose was so fancy, as if a mob boss had come out of the closet to perform on Eurovision. Did my father have affairs? I imagined him, abroad, having his pick of clever women, and rejecting them all, especially the butch German physicist at a wine bar in Düsseldorf he once mentioned. He was a tidy, small man and I was big for his suit, with the flares and lapels and turquoise stitching, but it would do. And it went surprisingly well with the trainers.

I had for therapeutic reasons got increasingly obsessed by bodybuilding after my daughter's diagnosis. The first night that I'd sung her Margol, one of my tears fell into her mouth as she slept. Five years later, I was in fighting shape, as the rabbi sang, "Let there be heard in the cities of Judah and the streets of Jerusalem the sound of joy." That morning, I'd kissed Liat on her forehead and explained that we were getting married because she was a princess and it was time for us to become King and Queen and, your mother beeping downstairs, I dragged out the metaphor, with mention of courtiers, witches and wicked mother-in-laws.

I watched you all drive off from the balcony. It was midday and I drank a coffee that had a limescale taint, dusty like the gravestones in the cemetery across the road, which was deserted, except for a man emptying the bin by the wash house. The dead were quiet neighbours, their marble markers, like plastic labels in flower pots, giving a name but not describing who they'd been. On wintry days, the stones jutted from the paved earth like rocks outside the harbour in Jaffa. I fancied the gravestones had been there for more than the eighty years since the first victims were buried after an outbreak of cholera. Sometimes, when I was cooking or listening to a play on the radio the cemetery appeared in the corner of my eye, like a strip of golden sand, walled off to protect the modesty of the sunbathing dead, with stumpy pines put up by the municipality to provide shade. The stones, inscribed with names, were like the city's dental records.

I had time to kill and, finishing my coffee, pottered over the road and for the first time in years went in. On the day I was to marry you, the sanest day of my life, I revisited the place where I'd cracked up. The sun made the back of my neck sweat as I looked at a line of graves for the men who'd died during the Jaffa riots of '21, including Yosef Haim Brenner, remembered primarily as a victim of murder rather than a talented artist. Others, like Haim Nachman Bialik, lurking at the lowest point of the graveyard nearest the sea, had found homes in concrete sepulchres.

The most imposing monument, because it stands taller than any other and is made of mourning black marble, is a memorial to the Jews of Zduńska Wola, in Poland, whose nightmare began slowly – strange accusations, intangible feelings of humiliation – until, in September '39, the Germans entered the village and torched the synagogue. The shiny black memorial stone was twenty feet high. I thought of Richard Strauss (a contemporary of my forgotten great-grandfather) and *Also Sprach Zarathustra*.

Goebbels called Strauss 'a decadent neurotic'. Strauss, for his part, tried to keep a low profile and the expedient behaviour got him appointed *Reichmusikkammer*, a duty he was relieved of in '35, after a letter to his Jewish friend, Stephan Zweig, was intercepted by the Gestapo. In it, Strauss asked bitterly whether Mozart was consciously Aryan when he wrote *Eine Kleine Nachtmusik*. What did the Jews of Zduńska Wola fear when it was announced on the radio that Hitler had invaded Poland? Could they have imagined that they'd end up names on a monolith in the middle of Tel Aviv? If we knew we were going to die, if we *knew*, we would kill ourselves, which is what I'm going to do when I stop writing. As Jean Amery said of Auschwitz, when death is certain it's the means of dying that becomes intriguing.

The Germans did not kill without moral purpose, but because they believed they'd discovered one. It wasn't nihilism, but thoughts of doing the right thing that made them gleefully execute children. And the radio, all the time, was used as the primary tool for transmitting the moral poison. Strauss, having written *Also Sprach Zarathustra*, would have understood the contradiction that murder was perpetrated because of a belief in the importance of life. He wrote shortly before his death in '49: "How can we feel so tired. Can this perhaps be death?" A tragedy lies in Strauss's too-late resistance: "The most terrible period of human history is at an end, the twelve-year reign of bestiality, ignorance and anti-culture under the greatest criminals, during which Germany's two thousand years of cultural evolution met its doom." Strauss had tried to save a Jewish daughter-in-law and his Jewish grandchildren.

I touched the stone and tried to remember the dead of Zduńska Wola. I hadn't included them in my doctorate, believing the case a tangential aside, but I'd got close to them during my research and am pleased I've found a place to include them here. And, remember, they lived opposite us. I saw them every morning, and I was reminded of what had happened. On our wedding day, I wanted to touch them and somehow, for some reason, thank them. Remembrance is what the memorial asked me to do.

Checking my watch, I wandered over to poet's corner, where the politicians Arlozorov and Dizengoff have situated themselves. Max Nordau's sullen mausoleum with its metre-thick concrete frame and metal door sealed with a rusty padlock has allowed him to brood in peace for years. Probably best that he was lying surrounded by bomb-proof concrete in the middle of Tel Aviv, hot, naked and sweating around him. His resting place is not unlike the Alice Gitter music library. He's happily blind in his cave, sulking away the after-life. At the Levant Fair in '32, when the first radio show was broadcast from Palestine under the authority of the British Mandatory Government, the city's mayor,

Dizengoff (I knocked a knuckle on his gravestone), expressed his desire that there should be a permanent station, a marker in the sand, to be known as Radio Tel Aviv. The sounds would travel to the corners of the universe: we are here, we are alive.

If only the Jews of Europe had managed to get within short wave of Palestine, to hear at first hand what was taking place, then millions might have been saved, but the British had other ideas. Radio Tel Aviv died the year before Dizengoff was buried. The children of Zduńska Wola found their deaths elsewhere. I realised how lucky I was to be standing in the cemetery. I decided, somehow, to get us plots under the willow. A wedding present so that we could be together here, a long time after, in death. Visiting the grave of Raziella Ben-Ari, I told her I was getting married.

"*Mazal tov,*" *she said.*

"*Thank you,*" *I said.*

"*Do whatever it takes to make her happy.*"

"*How?*" *I said.*

"*Forgiveness.*"

The mimosa bush was flourishing in the stony ground, sucking water from salty wells, tears that had once fallen on fresh gravestones, water from decaying flesh. It's yellow, smells bitter, and underneath it, close to the wall, shaded in the morning and the evening by the flowers, is Raziella's modest grave. I put a stone on it.

Emerging into the bright sunlight, I felt a wave of excitement and guessed I was ready to marry. The service was due to start at six. Our powder-blue Escort had rust under the wing mirrors and everywhere there were cracks in the paint-work. Rust had eaten a peach-coloured hole in the door, like the sunset in Haifa, the evening Shalom and I smoked our cheroots on the esplanade above the Bahai Temple on the ridge of the Carmel. Years later, in a Mane Katz exhibition at the Tel Aviv Museum of Art, I saw a similar sunset drawn at his studio on that same ridge in Haifa. My sunset had seemed infinitely more colourful. Katz's painting had it gloomy brown.

I drank wine from the rabbi's cup, to consecrate the final blessing. Your face glowed in the bulb-light and I couldn't wait to lift your veil and give you a wet kiss. The faces in front of the canopy were angled with affection. Saddam's missiles had proved a false alarm. No poison chemicals in their tips. And the summer had started early.

There's a photo hanging in a print shop in Ben-Yehuda Street, not far from the corner with Trumpeldor, of people gathered around a wireless radio store. They are dressed like they've gathered in Heldenplatz in Vienna before an evening of Strauss, too hot, those clothes, for Palestine, but that's where they'd found themselves. A pram with an arched hood and white-wall wheels and shiny spokes sits in the foreground seemingly abandoned. Young girls with slender legs and socks pulled up high, avidly listen to the announcement of the invasion of Poland on the 'Voice of Jerusalem'. I used to pass that store when I got off the bus from work at the university, at the corner of Trumpeldor, and get ambushed by the fruit-juice seller with a missing front tooth and a flat cap and, because I felt guilty that I was not born to listen to the radio in Zduńska Wola, and because of my gratitude that my parents left Vienna before Strauss was boycotted, I bought the biggest orange juice he had.

Missiles had rained down that spring and I'm sure they will again. Writing this, I can tell you that they have recently. One day, before I was born, the end of the world had been announced on the radio. Even on our wedding day, I was troubled. The past won't let go. The happiest day of my life, but still the shadows lurk, and I want you to understand that I'm not mad, it's just they're always there. The worst takes place. It did in '73. The best does too, and I took your hand and the rabbi bent over and placed a glass wrapped in silk on the stage. You encouraged me with a squeeze of my fingers. I slammed my foot down. I wish I'd got proper shoes.

I hopped about and kissed you. What sweet agony. People clambered onto the stage to congratulate us. I jumped about holding my foot and looked at the sole of my shoe. A shard of glass had stabbed its way into the rubber. Inside was squishy with blood. I accidentally put my foot down and screamed, and you rushed towards me. "Got a piece of glass in my foot," I said.

"We're supposed to spend some time together contemplating our marriage. Instead, I can bandage your foot. You're such a lunatic."

"I know. Don't think about it too much. You'll want a divorce."

In your mother's bathroom, you untied my shoe and my foot squirted blood. Your dress got spattered, but you pressed a tissue to my wound. "I'm sorry," I said.

"Don't worry."

"Your dress."

"It's only a little blood."

"I'm sorry," I said.

"What for?" you said.

"Everything."

"Nothing's happened. We're going to be fine," you said.

"Fine?"

"Fine," you said.

During the first dance, I stumbled twice. I was attempting to ballroom dance on a ruffed-up carpet on uneven ground on a foot recently knifed by glass, because of the symbolic act of remembering the destruction of the Temples in Jerusalem. I limped about the dance floor, having invested time and effort in classes for that very moment. I tried my best. I almost pulled off the tango.

I hit the drinks stand and the alcohol cauterised the pain, and we did the foxtrot. After the party, we went to your childhood room and made love on the small bed, surrounded by dolls and pink cushions. In the after-glow of drink and sex and dancing, I said, "Why did you do it?"

"It was a mistake," you said, and I wondered whether you'd have gone out with Shalom if he'd survived. He looked so different from me.

"It doesn't make sense," I said. And knowing what I know now, it didn't.

"I love you, Israel," you said. "Let's not talk. It's the drink. That was the best day of my life. Thank you."

I remembered Raziella's advice on forgiveness and muttered, "Din din nah trackadoo nah nah. Din din nah."

"You drank too much," you said.

"But you love me, don't you?"

"I do," you said. "And, for some reason, always have."

149

I've Got a Chance, Eviatar Banai

I've got a chance to be saved, I know. I could wake up, sober up. I could speak more, with love, about myself, about the city, about my wife. Even now, I'm less angry. A quiet wave of emotion has burst. The mother is singing to her child at night. Mother is here, by your side, all the time. I feel that something is changing. The exhaustion will pass and the light will rise. And I will recognise you, my darling. And immediately you will recognise me. I was always scared of going insane. That my heart will freeze and grow empty. But now that I'm sitting here. I've got a chance to be saved, I think.[17]

My best friend got minced by scorched metal, and my mother choked her agonised final breaths in a bed I used to jump on. However, I had Liat. She passed through tests: blood, cognitive, hearing and physical, all during her first week alive. The stethoscope picked up a heart murmur that sounded like the sea. She needed glasses but, until she was six months, couldn't fit them. I got my face close so she could touch my nose. She used to scratch it, and I used to nip her pot belly with my thumb. When we finally gave her green spectacles, she peered about my face as if she was putting together a puzzle or, as you said, "A scuba diver wondering at the stupid fish."

Her plasma showed up the extra chromosome. When we were told, you asked if they were sure, and I said, "Of course they're sure. You don't need a weatherman to know which way the wind blows."

"What?" you said.

"It's from a Zimmerman song."

"Who?" you said.

When we got outside, carrying Liat between us in a basket, after you'd repeatedly asked for twenty minutes if they were sure, I said, "I think it's great we know what's wrong with her. And the doctor says she's a mild case."

"Israel, I don't get why you're so upbeat. The way you range between anxiety and indifference is exhausting. Our daughter's very ill."

"Not ill," I said. "Just different from what we expected. But what did we expect? The fact that she's here is miraculous."

"I've never seen you so relaxed. You find it embarrassing to ask for directions. Now, you're all excited."

"I don't get me either. But look, she's smiling, isn't she?" I said.

"Yes. She's got a lovely smile," you said.

"It's yours," I said. "Most of the stuff that seems to be wrong with her are bits of me." You lit and sucked deep on a Dubek. "Taken that up again?"

"I'm stressed out," you said.

"Give me a sniff," I said, and closed my eyes and remembered the first day we'd met, before there'd been any real problems in my life, when I'd made myself as many as I could. I'd been too nervous to ask you to go for ice cream. When life's too good it makes me nervous about what's ahead, and I can always find something in the past to agonise over. When I have a true problem, like a disabled child to look after, I survive better.

Liat didn't stop throwing up. I carried her, on Yom Kippur,

through streets filled with children bicycling down the deserted roads, cocky, healthy brats, to the hospital, where it was decided, with great reluctance, to operate. She was only eight months old when they cut her open. It was my decision to let them. Luckily, the operation was a success. She had trouble recovering, but two months after, hands above her head, she cheered her rehabilitation. I watched her wake up and peer about and, putting her glasses on her, she clapped her hands.

"Yes," I said. "You're amazing. Ori come see this. She wants to play." You picked her up and carried her around the room, up and down, so that she giggled, and her hands missed on occasion but, set down again, she clapped with ease. "She's telling us she's going to be all right," I said, and noticed the pride in her eyes, so much like Shalom's. "You know who she reminds me of?"

"You?" you said. "She's crazy. Aren't you? Yes, you are. Crazy. My crazy little thing."

"Shalom," I said. "Did his ghost come back?"

"Stop it."

"Did the old stud came back from the after-life to help his friend out?"

"Stop humiliating me," you said.

"Only joking."

"It's not funny," you said, and marched off in a grump.

"Oops," I said to Liat, and took her hands and made them clap, but she was in a bad mood with me too. Her frown made no wrinkles, but I could sense the tension in her tight skin. "You should be proud," I said. "You're an angel." She'd inherited my blonde hair, and I thought it looked good on her. At one year old, she had the same amount as me. I blew the candle out for her, and she screamed. The sound of her excitement made my tummy spin. She knew she was the centre of my world. I was looking at her as if she was the vanishing point of the universe, filling that vacuum inside, singing to me from the spark-gap. You poured all your light into her and she was a happy, bright child. All those characteristics that I despised in myself were in her a glorious victory, the more awful, the more ennobling. She was hysterical, selfish, needy, competitive and stubborn, despite her condition.

That extra chromosome did have a purpose. She possessed demonic amounts of love. We gorged ourselves silly on how much she needed our attention and how much she could give in return. She wanted love more than anyone I've ever met, including myself, and I tried to give her as much as I could. Once she'd mastered *Kifkif*,[18] she could slap through a thousand and I had the patience as she chirruped along, *Kifkif – kifkif – kifkif – kifkif – kifkif.* The feeling of triumph in every touch of her damp palm gave me pleasure. She was trusting and, I think, mischievous. She once contrived to hide in the back of a drawer under some towels, until we found her laughing herself stupid. You were naturally disturbed by it, leaving me to revel in the role of being the calm one.

Down by the beach, when Liat was three, I was troubled because she couldn't crawl and wouldn't be able to enjoy splashing the water, like other children, so I picked her up and dipped her toes in the sea. Putting her down by our mat and umbrella for a nappy change, I turned for a second to blow sand from her sun hat, and was about to put it back on, when I saw her on her way to the water, speeding over the sand. She was using her heels to pull herself along, bum scraping the sand, leaving a furrow in her wake. I leapt up, but not wanting to distract her from her feat of athleticism and ingenuity, lingered behind, willing her on, cheering silently as she went, until she reached the water, and put one toe in. I heard her giggle and she clapped herself.

I called her monkey even though you thought other people might find it odd. When she laughed she got her mouth as wide as the macaque in my grandmother's book, *Das Tierreich*. I was delighted that her palm was a fortune-teller's nightmare. You couldn't predict the future with her; she had one line across her hand, known in the business as a simian crease.

At the age of four, her speech, which had been incoherent because of her over-sized tongue and under-sized mouth, became clearer after her new teeth came through, and she said, "Abba, why do you love me *tho* much?" The same day a man outside the grocery asked if it was tough bringing up a disabled child. My fist clattered his cheek, and he fell to the paving. Liat started crying, and I picked her up. "Monkey. Don't be scared. Abba's got a temper. When you're grown up, you'll see that I'm a bit weird."

She was shorter than the other children in her class and her movements awkward. But after her first outing to the Soldier's House Theatre to see Swan Lake, she swooped her arms like the Swan and tried to tiptoe on the carpet I'd bought from Eliahu. You had to admit that with a child the carpet was better than the tiled floor. Liat said, "I wanna be thtar!" Despite everything, she was going to be a performer, I thought.

"You're a star," I said. She gave me hope, and I took it selfishly. That evening, she was sitting in a pink tutu with her legs splayed, when I noticed something peculiar about what she was drawing. Below her – she always drew herself with a yellow head – was a blue circle. Above it, a bank of brown which had fireworks bursting in the space below the skyline. "What's that?" I said.

"The thee," she said.

"Where are you?" I said.

"On hill," she said.

I recognised what I was looking at. "Is it a sea or a lake?" I asked.

"Thee," she said.

"And what's that?" I asked, pointing at the brown ridge behind it.

"Mountainth," she said.

"And those, what are those? Fireworks?"

"No," she said. "Thilly."

"What then?"

"Boom-bangth," she said.

"Ori," I said. "Have a look at this."

"What have you drawn?" you said.

"Thee, and mountainth, and boom-bangth," Liat said.

"It's beautiful," you said.

"You know what that is?" I said.

"Why, what do *you* think it is?"

Liat circled her wax crayon on the paper and made explosion noises, turning the white red. "That's the view from my house," I said. "There's the Sea of Galilee. And that brown ridge is the Golan. The explosions."

"You're imagining it," you said.

"No, I'm not."

"Bang, bang, all dead," Liat said, looking up at me with Shalom's green eyes. I thought Shalom was talking through her, but kept quiet so as not to irritate you any more than I already had.

"Inherited memory," I said. "Shlomi was right. She's never been there. How does she know there were...what did she call them...boom-bangs?"

"You're imagining things," you said.

"No, I'm not. She's talented. There's something there. I'm going to get her a paint set." I did, but she never depicted anything like the view over the River Jordan onto Syrian artillery fire again. Encouraging her, I only had myself to blame when, having been distracted by a lecture I was supposed to be writing on 'The Civil Rights Movement and the Radio', I found the whole living room, and my beloved carpet, covered in blots of paint.

"What have you done?" I said. Her back was turned to me and she wiggled her bottom. "Oh, God. What a mess. You're in serious trouble." She turned around and her whole face was red, and I screamed, and she screamed, and I almost fainted.

"Sthtop it!" she said.

"You're in trouble," I said.

"You're in thrubble," she said. I grabbed her by the arm to lead her to the shower, and she said, "Don't kill me, Abba."

"Kill you?"

"Bang, bang, all dead," she said.

"Okay, we need to get you clean," I said.

"Woth funny, Abba?" she said.

"Nothing. You're in real trouble."

"So, why you laughing?" she said.

"Because… I don't know. You're as mad as me," I said.

"Mad?" she said, tilting her head quizzically.

"Or, I'm even madder than I thought I was. Come on."

"Come on," she said.

I took off her tutu and stockings and got her to sit in the water. I used wet wipes to clean her face, but it took ages to scoop the paint off. "Don't eat it," I said. She was chewing her lips like she had when she'd just been born. "Your mother's going to kill me."

"Kill you. Ha!" she said.

"Don't tell her," I said.

"Why you laughing?"

"Because you're so funny."

"Ith it a theekret, Abba?"

"Yes," I said. "I've got an hour to clean up."

"I'll help."

"No you won't," I said. "You're mischief."

"Mithcheef," she said, and laughed. Of course, you noticed the mess and said Liat could have been poisoned. I tried to explain that I was distracted by an interview that Rosa Parks had done on Radio KPFA in which she described how she refused to move seats. That broadcast rippled across America. We had our own problems in '56, but you got annoyed and told me you didn't want to hear about it. We didn't speak over dinner, although Liat and I shared sneaky glances. I think you suspected that I was becoming unhinged again.

We stayed in Haifa for my mother's funeral, and I thought of Shalom and how my mother's death, cruel though it was, had been expected. The garden was full of sub-tropical plants and the concrete fountain was dry. "Eden," Liat said.

"How do you know about Eden, my angel?" I said.

"Where I came from," she said.

"Really?"

"Yeah. You thed am an angel," she said.

"That's right."

"Grana likth gardenth."

"That's right," I said. "She loved watering her plants. What else did she like?" You dried my cheeks with your hand.

"Grath," Liat said.

"And what else?" I asked.

"Pijonth. Fatt pijonth," she said, banging her hands on my thighs and running about flapping. The air was cool that afternoon and we followed the trolley to the grave under oaks wrapped in clematis. "Thanks for coming, boy," my father said.

"I…"

"It's good to see you," he said. His face looked ragged. "She was ready to go, you know. Look after yourself, Israel. You were everything to her."

"I'll try," I said.

"Don't try," he said. "Schubert didn't get anywhere by trying. She was ready. She wanted to go. She's in a better place now."

"Liat says she's gone to Eden," I said.

The birds twittered to the prayer for the dead. Back at my parents' house, unchanged since my bar mitzvah, I worried about my father living on his own. My mother's passing was a fair capitulation to a treacherous illness. I wondered at all the memories that had been buried with her. My mother's story was submerged and I could only guess at the humiliations, the loss of friends and relatives, moving to Palestine, wars and domestic strife, peace and domestic bliss, sex and love, almost losing her son and a granddaughter with Down's. It meant something to me to know she'd once felt desire and passion. It's easier to make peace with the dead. I forgave her all those German words she'd muttered in the kitchen.

On Liat's seventh birthday, I remembered my first radio and how my life had changed forever. She looked at me, then around the room, and at you for prompts – you'd developed a symbiotic mind, so that telepathy gave Liat access to a second, encouraging source of ideas – but you wouldn't help her, feigning distraction by whistling. Without eye contact, Liat couldn't guess what you were thinking, and she said, "Erm."

"Erm. Is that all you want?" I said.

"She's really thinking this one through," you said.

"Don't pressure her," I said.

"I'm not," you insisted.

All I wanted was for Liat to get what she wanted, so I helped her. "Special dancing lessons?" Liat was tempted, but what I felt was going through her mind was that if she went for any one thing it would mean losing something else. Clever monkey that she was. "Erm," she said.

"Erm? What's an erm? Where can I get an erm from?"

"Thilly Abba," she said. "Thairth no thuch thing ath an erm." She looked at me to make sure she was right. She closed her eyes and made a wish and blew out her candles, gobbing all over the chocolate cake.

"What did you wish for?" I said.

"Nothing. I already got everything I want." We hugged, her wet hand on my back, the smell of your menthol breath, everything bound, arms, breaths, heart-beats. It's hard to bear the love we need to survive. That was the happiest moment of my life and it hurts to remember it. I'm not pretending that there were never frustrations with Liat, but when I think back on them, they were frustrations with myself. We won the double in '96, and I'd wrapped my yellow and blue scarf round Liat's neck. Bombs were going off in Jerusalem, and one in the Dizengoff Centre, where I took her to watch cartoons. It was shaking me up. Undressing her for bed, I told her to beware of suspicious objects and people.

When we passed a man, about forty, wearing sports shoes and a polo top with tracksuit bottoms flecked with paint, gesturing with a cigarette and shouting at a woman with a shopping cart – the woman was refusing to let him reverse his car out of the space he'd found on the pavement, because she was waiting for her bus in the shade – Liat pointed at the man and said, "Bomb."

I was embarrassed she'd picked up the wrong prejudice. "Not a bomb, monkey. He's one of us. A Jew. Don't worry, he's a Jew."

"Oh," she said, relieved. She'd heard me grumbling abuse at the television. That had led to this Jewish guy, a painter, rightfully shouting at the obtuse old woman with her white curls and jowly chops, being considered dangerous by Liat because of his skin colour. We shuffled along to buy fruit, both of us having a thing for what she called "thperthimmon," On her birthday that year, she said to me, "Can I visit grana in Eden?"

"First, decide what to do today," I said.

"I wanna danth. I wanna be famouth, Abba." My mother had tried to teach me to play piano, but I knew I'd never be Schubert, although I've ended up living longer than him. I'd consoled myself that in the long run Schubert will be forgotten, and in the very long run there will be no one to do the forgetting. But with Liat by my side, ego didn't need consolation. She could be a famous dancer, I was sure of it.

On our wedding anniversary, Liat came up and pretended to be a waitress taking our order. "What would you like?" she said. "Red or white?" After dinner, she brought the plates, a fork slipping to the floor, and handed them to me. Standing by me, she dried the suds. But when she started feeling unwell, later that year, she lost her confidence and said, "Whath wrong with me Abba? I'm funny looking."

"You get that from me," I said.

"No, ith like thumpthing went wrong before I woth born."

She died that winter, on a sunny day, in her sleep. During her first tests, they'd found a hole in her heart that kept her skinny. At first, she couldn't put on weight. You found it impossible to breastfeed her. After her operation, she took thyroid medicine and she'd got chubby, and then chubbier. I never found out how I'd have handled it when she started looking for love beyond us. I was saved from that. Heart failure the most logical cause of death, the doctor said, although he clarified, in cases like these, it's sometimes impossible to know why.

She was buried in one of the plots I'd arranged for us in the Trumpeldor Cemetery. For hours after we'd dumped soil on our daughter, we waited. We'd wanted no one there. No one deserved to be there, except for us. We'd loved her completely. But now she was gone, something had changed. I tried to put my arm around you. You recoiled and gripped the stone. I wanted you to find peace and tried to help you up. "Come, Ori," I said.

"Leave me alone," you said. The light in your face was out, my light.

"It's my fault," I said. "All this bad luck comes from me."

You gripped the stone. "Stop it, Israel. It's got nothing to do with you."

"I'm sorry," I said.

"Stop saying sorry or one day you'll be to blame."

I remembered Liat dancing with egg yolk on her chin and held the other side of the stone and now I'm no longer certain of anything, sitting here in my chair typing. I want to find you and Liat in Eden, but will I get there? I switch on the radio, hoping to find Liat saying, "Abba, why do you love me *tho* much?", but

162

instead there's an advert for foot cream. Then from the year she died Eviatar sings: "The exhaustion will pass and the light will rise. And I will recognise you, my darling. And immediately you will recognise me. I was always scared of going insane. That my heart will freeze and grow empty. But now that I'm sitting here. I've got a chance to be saved, I think." The radio always has something to say, however banal, it helps. I think I'm finally too old for pop music. I'm going to start listening to Schubert.

Soldier of Love, Eyal Golan

Pop music is the most responsive art form. It predicts, moulds, shapes and reflects the spirit of the age. It can only do that because of radio. Without radio-play, music is stagnant. Radio refreshes. Without radio, music cannot speak to its listeners. In the nineties, *Mizrachi* music bossed the airwaves. It became the authentic Israeli sound. I was delighted. Even though politicians didn't get it, and certainly the media hadn't a clue, the music was the people's choice, it said something about their mood. Sometimes a one-hit wonder bursts onto the scene, distracts, and moves on without impact. That's how Looly came into my life, as if from nowhere, she made me feel young again, like a good pop song.

Eyal Golan was singing on my Aiwa radio, his thin, rich voice, exemplary. Was he a young man singing old man's music, or an old man singing a young man's song in the style of old men? You get my drift, he was hard to place, and it's for that reason I love *Mizrachi* music. There's a timeless quality, so much yearning and longing behind the crude pop and lazy lyrics. Yet, in this song, he seemed to be yearning for something more obviously sad, a young man far from home asking his girl to wait, believing he's there to protect them both. I wondered whether you and I might set up our own station to transmit our love to each other, since we could no longer communicate. I imagined you in bed thinking warm thoughts about me though you never touched me with them. Golan was singing about war, his name evoking the place that Shalom had died.

My office was in the basement of the university. At the end of a corridor, beyond the toilets, a dead-end. Only the keenest seek me out and, being shy, they usually go away if I keep quiet enough. The room is about four metres by three, a cubby hole, but it has everything I want to read, re-read, in fact. A filing cabinet holds, in disarray, the information I'm required to keep on my students, grades and reports. There's also a bottle of Johnnie Walker in there. By the age of forty-five, I'd developed a need for afternoon snatches of spirit to revitalise myself, as my grandfather had with Calvados.

I no longer seek something original in books or clothes. I've stopped investing in fresh ideas. Intellectual fashions are teenage poses and slim-fit garments. I was never great at picking out avant-garde ideas in the first place. I like to swim against the intellectual current and with the people. I've lived long enough to know that fads are passing and that often the great works of the day stand counterpoint or in advance of academic group-think. While I was brooding in my room, like the spirit of Max Nordau grumbling in his concrete mausoleum, a delicate knock on the door repeated. I tried not answering, as usual. In fact, that afternoon, I'd taken special precautions. I'd slipped down the corridor having checked it was empty.

In my room, peering at the blossom on the trees and the acacia that shaded the car park and gave birds a place to perch and dirty the windscreens, I pulled down the blind, conscious someone could come around to check if I was in. Making sure I wasn't caught closing it, I thought, "Fatt pijonth." The Tadiran air conditioner, as old as I am, wheezed. I found myself stroking it and trying to shush it. A gentle knock, like a teaspoon tapping a boiled egg. "Shhh," I told myself as a picture of Liat, in her bib, came to mind.

"Dr Shine?" A light, precise voice. I turned down Eyal Golan, although it was impossible to hear it on volume setting three from the other side of the door. I'd experimented. Another knock on the door. The air conditioning had returned to its bass thrumming, camouflaged by birdsong. Another gentle knock, and I swung my feet off the table. I picked up my whisky glass and, opening the filing cabinet, hid it, and took out a pair of earphones that I draped on the desk. "Who is it?"

"Looly."

"Looly?" I said.

"From Zurich."

"Looly. I know," I said. "Wait a second."

I opened the door and, looking up at me, thin like a model but short, was a dark-haired, white-faced Swiss Jewess who spoke fluent Hebrew with precious vowels and clung to her Orthodox headband, for show, I suspected. "Can I come in?" she said, dropping her jaw with put-on disbelief.

"Of course," I said. "Had my earphones in. Listening to the radio. Recording by this great young tenor."

"Yes, I heard," she said. "Didn't think you'd be the Eyal Golan type."

"Oh. Right. Well. Do come in... Looly," I said. I hadn't factored in my poor hearing when testing whether you could hear volume setting three from the other side of the door. She ducked below my arm and her shoulder nudged my ribs. Her hairband, close to my nose, smelled of vanilla and allspice. She limped to the chair in front of my desk and, putting her hand on the filing cabinet, lowered herself with a stiff leg.

"What's wrong with your leg?" I said.

"Hurt my knee playing beach ball," she said.

"Do religious girls play beach ball?"

"Don't make assumptions. Not about students. Girls, especially. Religious ones, in particular. You make enough of them anyway. In class. Big ideas. You never explain them properly." I crawled behind my desk and switched off the radio. "Don't be embarrassed. Everyone loves Eyal Golan."

"Do they?"

"Yes, and you do too," she said. "You're like everyone."

"How can I help?"

She leaned forwards. "Sorry to bother you," she said.

"How very Swiss," I said.

"I'll try to be more direct."

"What do you want?"

"I want to do a Master's degree on the radio."

I looked for signs of sarcasm. You'd taught me, leading by example, to be suspicious of anyone showing an interest in the radio. At home, we knew my fascination was a form of therapy. Professionally, my colleagues thought I was a true academic, interested in the specifically obscure, even if at department meetings they kept my stipend under strict review. An MA student was exactly what I needed. You'd stopped working at the kindergarten. I felt guilty going to my father for money and, although we never went out, the rent in Tel Aviv was getting absurd.

"Are you all right?" Looly asked. Her eyes held mine with interest and sympathy.

"Why shouldn't I be?"

"You're sad, all the time. Can't you smile?" she said.

"A Master's degree?" I said, rubbing my hands. A silver stud in her nose caught the light. Her lips hung apart. The nose stud didn't fit the rest of her clothes: a long, modest pencil skirt, a white blouse buttoned up to her neck and the headband, holding down pinned hair.

"Why are you looking at me like that?" she said.

"Like what?"

"You're not blinking," she said.

"Neither are you."

"Because I'm trying to get something from you. My father told me to look people in the eye. It's supposed to be disarming," she said.

My neck was damp with sweat. I banged the air conditioner and put an eraser in my pen pot. The nose stud suggested libido. Why the disguise? What was true, the precocious sexuality or the modest dress, or both? She leaned forwards and giggled, and I told myself, "Don't be a fool." I thought that maybe I'd had a little too much Johnnie. Was I fantasising like an old man because I hadn't had close physical contact with you for so long? Looly played with her gum. "Want some?" she said.

"Looly," I said.

"What?" she said. "Don't you want some gum?" She blew a bubble.

"What flavour?"

"Strawberry," she said. "Do I have good enough grades to do a Master's in radio?"

"Why do you want to do an MA in radio?" The radio was far from obsolete, but I'd come to associate it with my own

169

fusty lecturing and dishevelled mid-forties decline, that I'd kept in check with continued visits to the gym. I told myself that I needed to keep healthy for when you rebounded from the painful mourning that you couldn't escape. The result was, I was in good physical condition. Perhaps Looly did want me.

"Are my grades good enough?"

"I don't know," I said. "Are they?"

"No, they're not. But they would be if you said they were. You can correct them. I took two courses with you. I didn't attend much or take the final exam, but if you give me nineties in both…"

"I'm not sure I can do that."

"I'll make the decision easier for you," she said. "I'm interested in the conflict between the new and the old, the adaptive technological resilience of some media in relation to others, survivability and initial reasons for discovery. Does an organism survive because it changes, or does it survive because it evolves to fit its environment? Radio, like people, seems to do both."

"Oo-aa," I said.

"I came up with it to impress you. It's something you said."

"It sounded genuine."

"Weirdly, I think it might be," she said. "I could be your daughter. Do you have any children?"

"A girl. She's not with us anymore," I said.

"I'm sorry."

I had to shake off the memory of Liat's hand on my back. "Do you really want to spend your life obsessing about radio?"

"I didn't know about your daughter."

"Radio?"

"I need to do a Master's so I can stay in Tel Aviv. My father's worried about the situation. Says it's going to get worse."

"How does he know?"

"It's easier to see from a distance. He thinks there's going to be another war. That's why our family moved to Switzerland. To avoid it. He can't understand why I want to get involved. I think it's too much fun not too."

"He's a pessimist, like me."

"A realist."

"That's what pessimists call themselves," I said.

"I want to stay, and I don't have the grades to do a more competitive course. I thought, since so few people attend your lectures, you might give me a chance. Give me a reason to stay, give you a reason to teach, give them a reason to pay. I liked your class on Radio and Fascism."

"I remember. But wait." I took out my class log. "You attended three lessons and didn't take the exam."

"Where do you think we are? Nine o'clock in the morning." She stood up, took the gum out of her mouth and put it in mine. "My grades." She leant on the table, arms bent concave at the elbows. I chewed and stared. "Dr Shine?"

"Yes," I said.

"Do I need to be Swiss about it? I was wondering very much if it was possible for a great man like yourself to use your impressive authority to make up some test results for me, so that then I could start work on an MA with a celebrated academic like yourself?"

"Yes," I said.

"Yes, you might?" she said.

"Yes," I said.

"I don't want you to get ideas," she said. "Some professors think every tiny girl that asks for favours is willing to give something in return. Would you like to teach me everything you know?" Her eyes widened on the word know. She took out a bottle of mineral water from her bag and handed it to me. It was warm and I imagined it salty like her skin. I rested the gum in my cheek and drank.

"I'll have to talk to the board," I said. "Financial problems. Can't promise anything. Who can? I would be delighted to supervise you. You've been a wonderful student all year and I will do my best for you. Thank you for coming and, if that's all, I'd like to be getting on."

"Getting on with listening to the radio. Another fix of Eyal Golan?" she said.

"Thank you very much for coming," I said.

I shuffled around her to the door keeping my eyes on the handle, opened it and smelled the sweet musk perfume when she passed. "No, thank *you*," she said, and gave me a kiss on the cheek. I stared at the floor and she blew in my eyes, like you'd once done straight from your menthol cigarette.

I was standing by the acacia, a week later, hoping one of my colleagues might give me a ride, when a silver Jeep pulled up and the darkened window hummed down. Tiny, in the beige leather driver's seat, was Looly. "Want to get in?" she said. "No one can see who's behind the dark glass. Cool, isn't it?"

"Very cool, Looly." I opened the door, climbed in and pulled on my seat belt.

"You going to say hi?"

"Shalom," I said, hands on briefcase on lap.

"Lighten up," she said.

"Okay," I said. "Can I turn down the music?" An agitated combo of syncopated drums and frenetic bass.

"Do whatever you like." Her hand left the automatic gear stick and patted my shoulder. "Where we heading?"

"Trumpeldor Street."

"Let's get a beer first," she said, and drove off at speed. We said nothing, mainly because I was breathless with anxiety. She parked on the kerb with a bump.

"You'll get a ticket," I said.

"They won't tow me from here."

"But the ticket," I said.

"I'll complain, they'll let me off. I'll say I had to stop because I forgot my prescription at the doctor's. I'm pregnant or disabled, or something. There's no parking in this city. They're liable."

"Where's your doctor?" I said.

"Who cares? There's a doctor every five buildings," she said.

"You'll want to get your story straight."

"They're not the Gestapo."

"No, but –"

"Come on," she said. "I don't have time. Got a date tonight. Just a quickie with you." I followed her into a cramped bar called the Lily Rose. The barman was cleaning the beer taps with window cleaner. "What do you want?" Looly said.

"Goldstar." It had been years since I'd been for a drink.

"Two," she told the barman with a victory sign. "Tell me," she said. "Have you thought about my proposal?"

"Not much, to be honest. Don't worry."

"I'm not worried." The frothy beers arrived. I grabbed mine.

"Hey?" she said.

"What?" I said.

"To life," she said.

"Forgot. Sorry. To life." I sipped.

"Hey?"

"What?"

"We're supposed to look in each other's eyes when we say that. We're supposed to mean it," she said, and we clinked. "What's wrong?"

"Nothing," I said.

"You're so sad."

"Yeah, well," I said.

"Please, don't be. When other people cry it makes me cry too," she said.

"I'm not crying."

"But you look like you're going to," she said.

"I'm not going to cry. Stopped crying two years and three months ago. People cry for attention. There's nothing left to cry about. And the only person I want to comfort is in too much pain."

"Your wife?" she said.

"Yes."

"Sad," she said, and put her hand on mine.

"I changed your grades," I said.

"Really?"

"Really," I said. "It was easier than I thought."

"Can I do the Master's?"

"You're down to do it," I said.

"You're my hero," she said.

"But I want you to promise me —"

"Promise you?" she said, grinning.

"Reassure me," I said. "That you really want to study the radio."

"I do. I want to study the radio, and to stay in Tel Aviv."

"You want to study radio in Tel Aviv?"

"Radio Tel Aviv."

"That's a good enough reason for me," I said. "That's all I want to do for the rest of my life."

"Not sure about the rest of my life."

"Who's your date with?"

"Omer, or Ofer, or Roy, or Omri, or Romi, or…you know," she said.

"I don't," I said. "I never dated. Does dating just mean sleeping around?"

"Don't know about that," she said. "Have to hope they pay for your drink first. I prefer meeting strangers in bars."

"I get that," I said. "Like accidentally falling in love with a record on the radio. Not having to go into a shop and work your way through the options."

"You're seriously obsessed," she said.

"I am. It's been years. I've done nothing else."

"When did you get that scar on your arm," she said.

"War. Before you were born," I said.

"Yom Kippur?"

"Do I look that old?" I said.

"Yes."

"Yes," I said.

I wiped froth from her lip. "Hey?" she said.

"What?"

"That's a bit forward."

"What did I do?"

"Touched my lip," she said.

"Because you had froth on it," I said. I'd cleaned her like I'd cleaned yolk off Liat.

"Nice move," Looly said.

"Time for another?"

"Not today," she said.

There was no ticket on her car. "You're a lucky girl," I said.

"Fortune favours the brave."

"No, it doesn't," I said.

"Where on Trumpeldor?"

"Opposite the cemetery," I said.

"Why doesn't that surprise me?"

I got out, in a hurry, slammed the door to avoid the awkward farewell and made it one, crossed the street, and climbed the dank stairs to our apartment. I opened the door with a gentle turn of the key and crept to our bedroom and found your body hidden under the summer duvet. I switched off the lamp, closed the door and strolled to the kitchen. The beer had me in a good mood and I took out chillies from the fridge and cut them fine with garlic, parsley and coriander. I shifted them into a bowl and soaked them with olive oil and vinegar. The fiery tang burnt my throat and had my eyes and nose running. I grabbed a milk carton from the fridge. I spent the rest of the evening waiting for you, but you didn't come out and at ten I slipped in beside you. You turned your back on me, and I said, "Good night."

After class, I was listening to some news programme detailing corruption allegations against the prime minister, a man with a similar sense of foreboding to me, based on experiences and memories, real or imagined, of the past. He of course had lost his elder brother. I was an only child, but I'd lost Shalom.

A knock on the door from a recognisable knuckle. "Come in Looly," I said.

"How did you know it was me?"

"You knock politely. So Swiss. Like the tick of a precision watch. And you're the only person who comes here," I said.

"What you drinking?"

"Whisky."

"Red Label?" she said, hands on hips, shaking her head.

"Yes," I said. "How can I help you?"

"Can I have some?"

"Help yourself," I said. She took the glass and, letting out her breath, filled her cheeks and swallowed the entire contents. "Hold on there."

"Don't worry, I'll buy you a bottle," she said. "Something good." She closed the door behind her and locked it. "This is bugging me," she said, taking off her headband, unpinning her hair and unbuttoning her blouse.

"Looly?" I waved my hands in front of my face. She unhooked and unzipped her black skirt. I could hardly breathe. "I'm an old man," I said.

"You're so sad. It's impossible not to want to help someone so sad." She crossed to my side of the desk, sat on my lap, no longer enigmatic, her nose stud and wild curly hair close to my face as her hot breath soaked my eyelids. Vanilla and allspice, her breathing rushed in pants between her lips. "You can touch me," she said.

"I can't."

"But you can," she said.

"How was the date?"

"Which one?" she said.

"I don't know," I said.

She laced her arms around my neck. "They're all boys," she said. "Cute, but idiotic."

"I love my wife," I said.

"Hurt both of us." I lifted her onto the table, she was light, her childish body intimidating, and sat back down. "It was worth trying," she said. "It's always been a fantasy of mine." She dressed and re-fitted the headband and became a modern orthodox girl again, with a nose stud.

I drew in a steadying breath and said, "Sorry."

"Don't be," she said. "Except for yourself. Which you clearly are."

"Can we talk about the radio?"

"I suppose so," she said. I nervously spoke about the nature of different radio frequencies and how they mesh and interchange. "What's that got to do with my thesis? I'm interested in how the radio is surviving. How it's staying cool. Especially when old men like you are involved."

We discussed how Napster had made its entrance onto the scene with something called an MP3 library that meant you could steal music and play it on a device with earphones. Looly said it was less innovative than the cassette, its only advantage being that you could download anything, and that music had become free. I argued it was not sharing music, as they claimed (we have the radio for that), but raiding people's creativity. However, some artists liked the flexibility of going straight to market, Looly said. I pointed out that there was no true market without the radio. Just individuals after what they could get. I worried that music without adverts lacked general aesthetic consent but agreed that according to statistics I'd received from the Israel Broadcasting Authority (IBA) listening figures were up, confirming her point of view, though I was sceptical. I wondered whether the statistics might be temporarily on the rise because the more of a good thing there was, the more people wanted it, in the short term, speculatively speaking.

She said, "I can't believe you didn't even touch me."

I ignored her and reasoned that perhaps music had finally become accepted as the universal art form and, therefore, there was enough space for a range of media to transmit, store, record and play. I had my doubts, but the radio was proving resilient. I hoped that analogue men like me had something over the digital boys. I told her that I was certain that the millennium bug would wipe away computers and MP3s and all the other inventions distracting us from each other. She said, "Of course it won't. Someone just wants money predicting a disaster."

I raised the fact that an interesting test case had occurred. *Arutz Sheva*, the nationalist radio station that broadcast from a ship in the Mediterranean called *Hatzvi*, in mockery of the already cited Voice of Peace (the radio's studios were in Beit El, near Ramallah), had been given a licence to broadcast by the Knesset, that February, and absolved of all its previous legal wrongdoings. The IBA was furious. What fascinated me was that this radio station was the first internet radio station in the world. It was used as a beta-tester for the famous RealPlayer streaming service.

Looly shrugged. "So?" she said. "There's loads of high-tech here."

It was odd though, I challenged Looly, that a Samarian village was responsible for something that I was convinced could save radio. How the mighty can be saved by the tiptoeing of zealous minds. "What?" she said. Saved the radio, I mused, by updating the transmission format but keeping the content. If there was hope for the radio, it was moving into this online world.

"I only offered to sleep with you because I thought it might cheer you up. But you're all excited about the radio and a settlement and the internet. You're such a geek."

"That doesn't sound like a good reason to sleep with an old man."

"The way you looked at me," she said.

"I've got a problem with blinking," I said. "And you're a beautiful young woman. Let's focus. I've been thinking about what you were saying before and I find it truly interesting."

"Oh," she said.

"Resilience, survivability and evolution."

"Is that what I said?"

"I think you put it better. But those were the headlines."

"It's incredible to me that the radio has adapted so well, that it has lasted, despite the obvious advantages of TV, CDs, DVDs, MP3s..."

"My thoughts exactly," I said.

"Hey, I have an idea."

"What is it?"

"I think the radio has survived because it's the most honest reflection of humanity in technological form. TV and film are obviously fake. Books are finished. What the radio gives us is the shared experience of the real. Cavemen in communities, struggling to survive, talking, making music, trying to predict the future, praying. That's what the radio provides us. It restores the ancestral function. It's like God has given us a way to connect back to who we were when he made us."

"Transmission through time. The creation dream. I couldn't have put it better myself," I said, delighted at Looly's sharpness.

"I've been reading your lecture notes," she said.

"The radio *reflects* humanity," I said. "You're right about that. In that little box we carry about who we are. The valves are the scrolls of the twentieth century and they'll be around forever. Hertz is our prophet."

"You're mad," she said.

"What's more," I said. "Everything that's been born since is purely an adaptation of the initial discovery by Hertz of those peculiar waves in our universe. The internet, GPS, wireless-internet. This new stuff is just an advanced manipulation of the old. The radio will live on, regardless. But what's interesting is, as you say, not only that radio recreated a world that had been lost, or that the radio waves are echoes of creation, but that the medium itself so coherently reflects the nature of its format. The radio is an atavism. It takes us back somewhere, the communion of lonely souls, tied together in time and space by bonds no less invisible and real than the electromagnetic energy that governs the universe. We are made from simple elements, but our souls are made from waves," I said. "Got any gum?"

"No. Sorry."

I stacked some books on my desk to make space and took out a piece of paper and sharpened a pencil. "On the matter of survivability, let us take the radio waves themselves before we take to task the fact that the radio, the thing, as you and I know it on a day to day basis, has strangely survived. Adaptation might be in its DNA," I said.

"Okay," she said, looking at the pencil with a heavy brow that darkened her eyes. Her mouth hung open and her cheeks fell in. It was possible she had an eating disorder.

"When radio waves encounter matter, in other words, when the ethereal hits earth, there are atmospheric changes and magnetic distortions. Their purity is contorted. Being plucked out of space and made to inhabit *in atmos* warps them. This takes place in numerous different ways: reflection, refraction, polarisation, diffraction and absorption. Should I go through each one?"

"Please do," she said.

"You're genuinely interested?" I said. "In the beginning was the…"

"Word…"

"And the word was…"

"God," she said.

"And how do you think that word could be sounded in a vacuum?" I said.

"Maybe it wasn't sounded," she said.

"Presuming it was, it must have been sounded from something inherent in the chaos.[19] What was that chaos? The scrambled electromagnetic waves that needed to be untangled so that the word God could be heard. In other words, before God said, 'Let there be light', there had to be sound, transmitted on radio waves. That little box." I pointed at the Aiwa and continued, "It uses the same means as God to communicate. It has the universe inside it. What was I saying?"

"You said, *Should I go through each one?*"

"Let's get these down on paper. I'll draw them for you. Reflection, that's simple. Waves bounce off other objects. That's how humans learn. Watching others, our souls bouncing back to create a modified wavelength. Refraction is the distortion caused by being forced to pass through another medium. We might call that a form of moral corruption. Polarisation bends light waves into a flat beam."

I looked at the squiggles on the paper, put the pencil down and said, "Diffraction, and I find this one the most compelling, as it accords with some psychological ideas I was once introduced to, is when a wave passes through an aperture and ripples out. To me diffraction is a metaphor for our birth. That moment at our beginning is really the middle, the aperture in space-time that our soul squeezes through to find existence. The resulting distortive effect is that our souls bring with them moments that we've never experienced but make us who we are. That's why it's so difficult to work out who someone is. We're a single soul, a wave, diffracted into concentric circles." Looly yawned and I said, "Last one. Absorption. In brief, that's how we mediate ourselves through love and attenuate our spiritual energy within someone else."

"Romantic," she said.

"Am I boring you?"

"Yes. Because you're too theoretical. And you do all the talking," she said.

"Because there's something impossible to define about all of this," I said. "It's like having a fight with a ghost."

"Wrestling with time," she said.

"Old men do that."

"When you were talking, now, you were so enthusiastic. Even happy. I wish something or anyone could excite me like that."

"You're young," I said. "Imagine what it's like when you get to my age. Life's illusory, like the blue sky, you can't hold onto it. We're grappling with ideas designed to be too big for us to understand. Imagine those space-walkers staring at the earth. The prophets gave us an aperture, a moment of clarity, that shows us there is something beyond. Striving to get close to that vision is the closest you can get. That's what a great song does to you. That's why Heinrich Hertz was such a seer. He opened the universe, the one that already existed, with the imagination that God had given him. Maimonides was right.[20] The universe couldn't have been created out of nothing, because there's chaos before the word. And prophets are not chosen by God, but allowed by him. Hertz discovered the rhythm of the universe, the cycle of frequency that we named after him. He invented the medium and the message. That's why the Nazis went after his bust. There was God watching them. But you're right. This is all too theoretical. We need to understand what we've used the radio for. I'm talking too much, aren't I?"

"You're exhausting."

I saw in her perplexed boredom a sensible reluctance to engage with abstractions, being, as they are, intangible like radio waves. She'd already stopped trying to see, because she believed we were doomed to be blind, and she was right. "I'll lighten up. I promise that it'll be your theories that I'll listen to. But I think the medium is worth it. I think we're lucky you decided to knock on my door." How could I have thought that? The last thing this young woman needed was my old-man fixation.

"I should get going," she said. "I'll see you next semester."

"Yes. Do. I'll work out a framework of secondary reading."

"Thanks," she said, and rushed off. A clever girl, too clever for academia. I saw her Jeep at the traffic lights once, but never saw her again. What did you think? I'm a foolish old man, but not that foolish. I'd never have cheated on you.

White Christmas, Destiny's Child

It's like you've lost buoyancy, down there, lying in the dark, sweaty sheets barely holding you together. You don't believe in light. Breathing is hard, automatic and tiring. You'd spent so many hours of your day in bed, emerging to look for a distraction: frozen snacks for the microwave, cleaning the sink, opening letters. We barely spoke.

Eventually you floated up. You, my light, one day, without warning, smiled at me. The summer had been quiet, and I think that helped. I was working on my 'History of Radio'. Same problem as the thesis. I was good at collecting anecdotes but relating them proved agonising. I passed afternoons in my chair reading and crunching on apples. I'd pour myself a vodka and grapefruit at seven. Boil rice for you. The fluffier the better. If the bowl came back unemptied, I felt angry with myself, I imagine like a mother who cannot suckle a child.

"Eat, Ori," I said. You sat up in the dark and took the fork from my hand and ate. I stroked your back, where it was downy, at the bottom.

In early September, you rolled over and said, "Israel?"

"Yes?" I could hear the lightness in your voice. "I can see you in the dark."

"I can see you," I said. "You're smiling." I pressed your nose. "How are you?"

"Fine," you said. "I sound like you."

"How?"

"Saying fine, when everything's not," you said.

"Saying fine helps," I said.

"That's true. I always thought you were going to get better when you said it. Meant you could deal with things," you said. "Did I catch this depression off you? Do you think there's a theory about that? Infectious psychosis or something?"

"You're grieving. Nothing abnormal about that. You're the sane one. You're healthy."

"That's what you always said about yourself. Sane in a mad world. I sometimes thought you were right. But how long should we grieve for? When does it stop being grieving and become your own slow death? Liat's been gone for years and I can't do anything without her. I can't teach other children. I resent them."

"You're fine."

"There you go again," you said.

"But you are," I said, and picked your squidgy hand off the sheet, and you pulled yourself up the headboard. You'd put on weight despite the depression. I'd had the same thing with the Lotus biscuits. You'd eat *burekas*²¹ in bed, between attempts at vegetables and rice.

"Not sure I am," you said. "But I want a coffee. How long's it been?"

"A long time," I said. "How do you want it? Milky?"

"A little," you said.

"Okay, one coffee for you. I can't wait to put the kettle on," I said, and bounced off the bed.

We went for a walk together. You wore a pair of shorts and a vest. I held your hand until both of ours were sweaty. I showed you all the places I'd been the day I'd broken down, except the masseuse. I didn't want you knowing about that. At the entrance to Trumpeldor Cemetery, you took a deep breath and I said, "One small step…"

"Why do you want to go in here anyway? I've always avoided it and when you went crazy it proved me right and when Liat…"

"Come on, let's go visit her. She'll teach you not to worry," I said. "Look at that willow."

"Oak," you said.

"Willow," I said. "There's another space under there I'm going to get for us so that we're all buried together."

Your hair had lead-grey shoots at the root. "Death and love go together. I don't think I can see her yet."

"Another day," I said. "I read in some cemeteries they're stacking graves vertically. Luxury towers for the dead. Lucky your husband planned ahead."

"You look lovely," you said.

"So do you."

"You agree you look lovely then?"

"Can't imagine what it must be like to have spent your life looking at my head."

"I like it," she said.

"Still," I said. "What a way to spend your time."

"I hope I'll be looking at it for years." The older graves had shifted with the ground and we came to a dead-end where we had to climb over a headstone to pass. "Poor people," you said.

"They're not here," I said. "They're radio waves. Liat is flying around the stars."

Out on Ben-Yehuda Street, I bought you a fruit juice from

the man with the cap. "Didn't that used to be Pub Lick?" you asked, pointing across the road.

"Don't know."

"Yes, it did," you said. "What's it called now?"

"Bar Fly," I read off the canopy.

"Funny," you said. "It all seemed so important at the time. I thought I'd lost you for good. Can't believe you hit him."

"Why did you want me in the first place?"

"You brought me that pack of Dubek," you said.

"You didn't smoke them."

"It was the kindest thing anyone had ever done for me. You were so awkward. You needed saving. I wanted to be the one to do it."

"And you did," I said, taking your hand on the corner of Gordon Street and leading you across the road. We passed under the concrete L-bends holding up the Ramada Hotel and down onto the pebble-dash swirls of Mayor Lahat's promenade.

"Ice cream?" I said.

"At last," you said. "Just for you. Because it's hot."

"What flavour would you like?"

You assessed the options. "Didn't know you can get Mars or Maltesers."

"I'm going to get strawberry," I said.

"Of course you are. You used to feed Liat strawberry ice cream. But she hated the flavour, *sthtrawberrieth, yuck*."

I put my arm around you and kissed you in the parting of your hair, the smell making me feel at home, but sad. "Ori?"

"Yes," you said.

"Are you going to be all right?"

"I don't know, Israel," you said.

"Get two scoops."

"You think it will help?"

"In my imagination it will."

"Mars and Maltesers then."

Under the hotels, people were playing bat and ball with gloves, taking the game seriously. A leathery old man leapt across us and pelted the ball at his partner. You stumbled into me, and I supported you with my chest. The boats in the marina were clinking in the wind and seagulls barked about the bins of a fish restaurant while trying to avoid the cats. The sea came close by the headland, and I remembered Shalom and I carrying our crate of Goldstar.

"I'm only forty-seven but all I've got is memories," I said. "Nothing changes, everything changes, nothing stays the same but everything does. Can't we make more memories? Don't we have it in us?"

"Liat was our future," you said and you were right, but it seemed so premature, even then, to be nostalgic because we'd lost our daughter. Did you know then that we didn't have that long left? Another decade or two, and then what? Most of our meaningful lives were behind us.

"We're like an old couple," I said.

"I'm lucky to have you."

"Me you," I said.

"We can be lonely together," you said.

I took your empty ice cream cup and binned it. You puffed on a cigarette, and I breathed in the cool mint. There was hip-hop music coming from the beach bar at the head of the sand where I'd spent the day with Aya. "I came here once with Shalom," I said.

"Here?" you said.

"Yes."

"Can I tell you what happened?" you said.

"Okay," I said.

"He came to find me. Those green eyes and thick eyebrows. He told me I was lucky you were interested in me. That you were the most beautiful man he'd ever met."

"Did he say that?" I said.

"I didn't know who he was talking about. 'Blondie', he said. I knew it was you. You with the Dubek. He said he didn't know why you were interested in me when you could get anyone."

"Sounds like Shalom," I said. "Same tactic every time. Attack the best form of defence."

"I was upset. He put his arm around me and told me to cheer up because at least you weren't going to die. You weren't going anywhere, he said. I didn't know what he meant. He told me that he was going to die. I asked why he thought that. He said he knew there was going to be a war and that he trusted you. The colonel that took me into his bunker, the one who tried it on, confirmed it."

"Is that true?"

"Shalom told me that he was going to die and that I had to promise two things."

"Two things?"

"The first was to marry you. I told him to stop being ridiculous. But first, he said –"

"He wanted to be with you first?"

"Listen. First, he said that if he died, and he knew he was going to, I had to promise him that I'd tell you I'd slept with him so that you wouldn't miss him. So that you'd hate his guts."

"What?" I said.

"I didn't for years. But then, by the flower stall, I remembered him saying it because in my office there was that bunch of white tulips. Do you remember? They died before the first shot was fired because no one had time to water them."

"Yes," I said.

"And so, I told you, finally, that I'd slept with him. I was so scared that you were going to reject me. But I knew how much you loved Liat. And I wanted to do the right thing, finally, by Shalom."

"Yes," I said.

"I told you and you said –"

"Marry me," I said. "We'd never have got married without him. He gave me the strength to do what was right. From out there, somewhere in the ether. You never slept with him?"

"I never slept with him," you said.

I sat down on the pavement, with the hip-hop beats, bicycles circling round me ringing their furious bells, and put my head in my hands. "I knew it," I said.

"I know you did," you said. "But I didn't want to break my promise. Not to a dead man. I can see his eyes when he told me he was going to die. I told him it wasn't going to happen. But I'm too tired for promises to the dead. Liat has gone. He's gone. They don't exist. I know that. Which is why this morning I decided to get up. I couldn't tell you straight away. That's it."

"We wouldn't have got married without him," I said.

"We might have," you said.

"I'm a coward without him."

"I'm sorry," you said.

"What for?"

"Everything," you said.

Our stories had become intertwined, you and I, bit by bit, tied together, memories bound by love. I knew that without you, I couldn't survive and I know the same, right now, writing this memoir. That's why I'm going to kill myself when I finish. "What would I do without you?" I said.

"Listen to your radio," you said.

"You're probably right." We climbed up the steps to Independence Park, where rubber plants had red petals, and down the other side, holding hands, until we got home. I poured us two grapefruit and vodkas, we needed them, and I sat down while you made me dinner.

Three days later, the Twin Towers. The panic caught in my throat. The cycle of pictures got to me and I considered it the beginning of the end. Writing in silk pyjamas, on a sultry day, nineteen years later, I realize it's a slow-burn conflagration. How much longer can we survive the hate?

As the towers turned to ash, we had our own fires to handle. I was playing solitaire, and turned the Queen of Clubs, when a blast rattled the window. A bomb sucks the air out. Twenty-one children killed on the beach waiting to get into a night club, their bodies scattered into the air. I couldn't walk by the mosque opposite without my breath catching on the wind, and changed my evening stroll, by going up Ben-Yehuda and across at Gordon, past the art galleries, the way I'd gone with you.

In Jerusalem, fifteen people were slaughtered for eating pizza. Their bodies ripped to gore as they waited for their toppings to melt. A two year-old's head was pulled off by the explosion; shrapnel and semtex, hidden inside a guitar case.

Eleven more shopping, annihilated, fifteen more on a bus in Haifa, massacred. A year of cripples, the disfigured and dead, and there was no answer to it. As Ori got better, I found myself getting worse. My background reading for my 'History of Radio' had taken a maudlin turn and I was looking, again, at jazz in ghettos, concentration camps, and in Paris, during the war.

I hadn't lost hope in radio. Somehow the other side would hear what was happening to us. But the other side were using two-way radios to avoid detection. In Paris, by the end of '39, a quarter of all radio play was jazz. A youth movement began in Montmartre and Saint Germain. The rebellious youth became known as 'Zazous', a Johnny Hess lyric from a song called 'Je Suis Swing'. When in '42 the Jews of Paris were made to wear yellow stars, Zazou protesters wore similar stars with the word 'swing' cut out or inked in the middle.

For good reason, the Germans associated swing jazz not only with 'Negroes' but with what they termed 'Jewish subhumans'. One of the continental swing masters was a Jew from Prague called Fritz Weiss. He and his family were sent to Theresienstadt. The SS invited the Red Cross to visit the camp and Weiss played Benny Goodman on his clarinet. Once the propaganda was complete, Weiss, his band, his family and thousands of others were sent to Auschwitz. Weiss chose to accompany his elderly father into the gas chamber.

"Israel, stop shouting. It won't change anything," Ori said.

"No?"

"No," she said. "It won't change anything."

"What do you think we're going to do about it? Why can't people see evil? What's wrong with them? Why don't they believe it exists?"

"Something will be done," she said. "There are lots of people who feel like you and they'll do something. Now, switch it off, it's not good for you."

It wasn't just the news getting to me. My father was in hospital, a shrunken seventy-seven, hair torched by chemo (lightning does strike twice), his head cranked on his shoulder, spit leaking from his mouth. I kept him clean, returning the long-ago favour, but he wasn't a child, it wasn't fair for him to have lost his dignity, a man that gave dignity such value.

He was bone and skin. Cancer is your body killing your body, cannibalising itself, nature against nature, the most unnatural natural death, the strangest of genetic screw-ups. Even Liat hadn't gone through what my father and mother had. He'd been diagnosed as terminal in April. He patted my hand when I visited, instead of the other way round. "Well," he puffed out of lungs already under pressure from the growth. "I guess that's it."

I'd moved him to Tel Aviv, to be near him, and because there was an expert gastric oncologist at the Ichilov hospital. He didn't get on drugs trials because of his age, and I was furious, but it turned out everyone on them died. Outside the hospital window, grey clouds fled the horizon. Rain washed away the summer, slugs climbed damp concrete, dust and pollution drenched the gutters, and the air smelled of wet grass. You'd returned to cooking, though not to school. You baked salmon, and I went to the gym twice a week and lectured at Tel Aviv University on my favourite subject, the radio and anti-Semitism.

I needed to lighten my workload so that I could concentrate on researching and writing my book. With Tel Aviv University on my resumé, I thought I'd get published within the year. I'd had preliminary conversations with their in-house mark, and it sounded to me that only my own failure to get the work done would stop publication. That was no small obstacle.

In the wave of terror that broke over the land, I decided to imitate the Zazous in Paris and listened to 88FM Jazz, hoping to make myself a better person. Technology had improved against the backdrop of renewed butchery. Mobile phones were ubiquitous. iPods stored all the music you could want. Amazing technology, beautifully designed, but lacking the purity of the radio, which kept on playing.

There were some great songs that year, but the record that stood out, at the end of it, was 'White Christmas'. It came on unexpectedly as I was driving to see my father in early December through sheets of angry rain, sung by a girl band called Destiny's Child (the lead singer had a competent voice), and halfway through, falling into an R&B funk, I thought it did very well capturing the grotesque nostalgia of the melody, lyrics and timing of the original. Something in my gut turned and began to grow. Soon, my whole body was filled with rage.

Inside the cancer ward, the light coming through thick clouds past blue-tinted windows was easy on the eye, and I looked out over the city that was sprouting narrow skyscrapers from wet pavements. I hoped my father would see another spring but, looking at him, it felt unlikely, his body curled, saying "Enough". I'd bought him an iPod and let him hold it for comfort, having downloaded all of Schubert's *Lieder*. There was one that particularly got to him. He tried to move the gadget into his line of vision. Going over to him, I leant my ear to his mouth and he whispered, "Schu…" I skipped back to the beginning of the track and his head relaxed into the pillow. I asked him if I could listen, one earphone each. He didn't say no.

For men like my father, committed and stable, the radio lacked focus. How could he possibly hope that the radio would play the *Lieder* he wanted when he needed it? For Sixties children, there was no chance of listening to songs by Arik Einstein or The Churchills without the radio. To collect recordings, you'd need endless patience and money. If you're happy with Schubert, a record collection will do. The point about the radio is that it reflects in sound where you are in space and time. My father had never been where he was. Listening to Schubert in that hospital bed, he found a place before he was born where he'd have been happy. An inherited memory, I thought. His soul was refracting.

The sound quality from the iPod was very good and I wondered if the radio might finally count itself out. Were we set to become lonely possessions of little machines? I was forty-seven and, having grown up with the radio, I feared the radio, like me, was defunct. But inside the iPod, there was no spark-gap, no universe, no space for us to share. The future was isolation, but a future my father could have enjoyed, since the past he dreamed of was stored inside.

It's a shame he wasn't more like me, and I more like him. I found German a clumsy, violent language. I'm ambivalent to the romance of the *Lieder*. Not my father, closing his eyes as the tenor catcalls. The fact that my father wanted one song, specifically, encouraged me. Despite the pain and dulling effect of morphine, he'd a choice to make and could make it.

The music seemed to wander and, not fully understanding what was being sung, I watched my father. He smiled at "*Zaubert Blumen aus dem Schmerz*". And at the end, sighed to "*Hört in Lüften ohne Grausen. Den Gesang der Geister brausen*". He opened his eyes and I leant over his mouth and he tried to say something,

"Schu…" He swallowed, but the obstruction didn't move. I watched him gulping with fazed concentration. He calmed, and I leant in. He whispered, "Schubert was thirty-one." I felt him pushing his hand into my palm, his chest throbbing, his face grimacing, but I knew it was because he was laughing. I rubbed my hand in circles on his chest.

"Shhh," I soothed him.

"Again," he said.

I flicked back to the beginning, and off we went through the Austrian forests of his childhood that my mother had called the *Wienerwald* on our trip to Metula. He closed his eyes, and I imagined him playing swords among the trees and wearing green trousers and a frilly shirt. Later, when I returned home to Haifa, I went through his photos and found one of him, a happy Austrian child. I'd known he'd looked like that, though I never knew the boy that became this man in hospital, my father. He was, after all, with his Schubert *Lieder*, an Austrian from Vienna, but it had never interested me enough. I never took the chance to ask him what bringing me up in the Galilee felt like to a man brought up in a city in Europe. It's not the first time I'd failed to do the right thing, or ask the right questions.

It's funny that at the end of his life, he continued to flee back to that imaginary space created artificially by his parents, the childhood to which we all return, protected as we are, for a short while. In the life that comes later, the artificial refuge of childhood seems most real and, when we close in on our deaths, we reach towards our births. I stroked my father on the cheek and said, "We both outlived him."

"We did well," he said, trying a smile. Exhausted by the effort, he whispered, "Again." I pressed play. His breathing was light, and I didn't notice it stop. His brow twitched once to the music. By the end of the song, only my father's body was lying in front of me. He'd gone elsewhere. At the speed of light. His soul, another radio wave fleeing through space. Schubert's music, written so long ago, had taken him with it. I hoped his last thought, which would be his for eternity, would be of home, and I wished that it was not Austria, but with me in the Galilee, where he'd taken me for walks by the lake, pointing out flowers that reminded him of another life.

I found *House of Dolls* behind Bialik, and Spinoza's *Ethics*, on the top, back row of my father's library, the week he was buried. The mess of books stacked on wood shelves, buckling under the weight of paperbacks piled vertically and horizontally (if they'd been of recent interest to him), had hidden the book that I'd forgotten about, except obliquely during Shlomi's inkblot tests. The picture on the front was of a woman seductively opening striped pyjamas onto cleavage, her delicate jaw caressed by clean hair.

It was an account of a sex-slave in Auschwitz-Birkenau, but it was published in a way that was intended to be alluring. The author had a nonsense name, K. Tzetnik. I had the feeling that I could share something with my father by reading it. The author's name, according to the inside cover, came from the German acronym for *Konzentration Zenter*. I sat outside on the lawn by the concrete fountain, the appraisers putting stickers on the furniture inside, and the pigeons circled around me.

I came across words I knew too well: *lager, ghetto, Gestapo*. I'd read this before: "*Nobody knows what Auschwitz is. People vanish into it without a trace*". And now, writing my memoir, and considering how I want you to see what I cannot show you in

198

words, I repeat what I'd read more than once: "*All sorts of photographs. So many photographs. Big ones and small ones lie scattered over the floor and people walk on them*". The heroine of the story, Daniella, "*plans her trip to Palestine*", but is sent with the rest of her city to Auschwitz before she can leave. She is saved selection, a "*chance occurrence*". For Daniella, "*It was the first time she'd ever seen Germans*". Auschwitz was built upon the Jewish town of Oshpitzim, where travellers lodged at Hotel Hertz. I wondered whether Heinrich Hertz had been related to the hotelier. Not impossible. No doubt the declaration of war had been broadcast on the radio set up in the lobby.

In Daniella's hut, those left were the fortunate few who slipped the "*aktions*". I remembered falling in love with a girl called Fella, "*her twin rows of sparkling laughing teeth…she was hardly along in her teens when men were already flocking around her*". I was titillated by the murky sentence: "*They really went to town at the militia last night and the bastards didn't lay off Fella all night. Didn't even let her catch her breath*". I remembered lying in my bed with a torch as a young boy, glimpsing words I didn't recognise, understanding something terrible had happened. Was it the night before I caught my parents having sex? Had I imagined or dreamed what I'd seen through the dusty glass?

"*The Gestapoman is holding a list in his hands. Death has ordinary, white, human hands*". The girls are taken in cattle cars, past corpses strewn in a mass grave to another camp, "*Arbeiten via Joi*", and the electric stamp tattoo, "*Feld-Hure*". I'd read this book and suppressed it. Did I project German onto my mother's lips? Before becoming a sex-slave, Daniella felt, "*the scorching heat that had been burned through her vagina. In the rows of cages opposite were girls whose experiments lasted for extended periods: artificial insemination, twin insemination, miscarriages, premature deliveries and various methods of castration and sterilization… Daniella lay naked, her parted knees still strapped to the iron rods at both sides of the table. In the hand of one of the assistants, she saw the same instrument which they had, that morning, inserted deep into her vagina. He looked at her with her excised organ floating in a jar".*

The next day, Daniella became an active member of the band of emptied women, the 'Joy Division' who lived in the 'Dolls' House': *"Every day, at two o'clock, German soldiers, on their way to the Russian front, came from the nearby transit depots to entertain themselves. If the guest was not satisfied, he could report it. Three such reports and the doll was killed".* If the bed was not the requisite four inches above the frame, death, if you didn't smile at your rapist, death, if you didn't pretend to enjoy being raped, death, if you didn't in some way satisfy, you were taken, nude, and executed. That was the 'Joy Division'. It upsets me as I write, that some punk fools could call their band by that name. How could there be a group from Tel Aviv called, 'The Dolls' House'? Sometimes, the radio colludes in the evil of young men.

I returned to Tel Aviv in a car packed with my father's books. I made another effort to understand. I read and barely slept. Irving Berlin's schmaltzy masterpiece went round and round my head sung by Destiny's Child. The sentimentality of 'White Christmas' is not the opposite of evil, it denies it. Berlin knew how dark his white Christmases had been and he lied, and he knew that he was lying. He understood what was happening and decided that the only way to escape was to fake, be saccharine, produce sentiment. What was he feeling when he wrote, "Where the treetops glisten and children listen to hear sleigh bells in the snow?"

Berlin's response to evil was charmed indifference. To believe in the redemption America offered, he had to wipe out the memory of the world he'd come from. By re-inventing a history of idyllic Christmases enjoyed with the kind of romantic Northern European charm that was a prerequisite for the collective madness of National Socialism, he took part in the denial of truth that allowed the Holocaust to take place. The pogroms had been warning enough. But he doesn't mention Cossacks murdering and raping Jews on Christmas in the White Russia of his childhood. His tear-in-the-eye nostalgia for better, whiter times not only covered up reality, it reinforced a new one.

Berlin was lying, in '42. When the Mufti offered Hitler his "thanks for the sympathy which he had always shown for the Arab and especially Palestinian cause, and to which he had given clear expression in his public speeches. The Arabs were Germany's natural friends because they had the same enemies as had Germany, namely...the Jews..." Don't talk about it. Listen to the sham that's 'White Christmas'. The facts are offensive. Here are some from '42 that I can't put aside.

The New Year opened with a fizzle; Zyklon-B was dropped in at the red farmhouse at Auschwitz-Birkenau. Delighted with the results, the bigwigs at the Wannsee Conference decided on their Final Solution. During Lent, the Belzec extermination camp got going. The first trainloads of Parisian Jews arrived in time for Passover. Did Berlin get his copy of *The New York Times* over *Shavuot* when it was reported that one hundred thousand Jews in the Baltic States had been shot into burial pits they'd dug for themselves, and a further one hundred thousand in Poland, and twice as many again in Russia? The second gas chamber at Auschwitz opened on the day of Jewish national mourning, *Tisha b'Av*, to handle the plenitude arriving. In the heat of a New York summer, as Berlin was bizarrely writing 'White Christmas', did he read that one million Jews "at least" had been killed "so far"?

Jews from Berlin sent to Theresienstadt. Dutch Jews to Auschwitz. Deportations from the Warsaw Ghetto to Treblinka. Belgian Jews to Auschwitz. Croatian Jews follow. All Jews left inside Germany to Auschwitz and Majdanek. The mass killing of Jews from the Mizocz Ghetto in Ukraine. Deportations of Jews from Norway to Auschwitz. The first transport from Theresienstadt arrives at Auschwitz as Christmas is approaching. Snowflakes melting on the busy railway line as one hundred and seventy thousand Jews around Bialystok are put to death in time for a white Christmas. It had not been a good year, whatever the mood Berlin's jingle puts you in, and that was why I was distracted by the song being played as you told me what you'd done with Shalom. There are some things worse than what you'd covered up. Think of Berlin's level of deception. And, as it turned out, you'd never slept with him anyway.

We'd said little after the proposal by the flower stall. Liat clapped her hands in the back seat. You snorted when I started singing, "I'm dreaming of a White Christmas, just like the ones I used to know", raising my hand dramatically from the wheel. I approached your father, after dinner, and received his blessing with an embrace.

After my father's funeral, you made me meatballs with eggplant. You'd avoided the burial for your own sanity. I started on my father's collection of books that I'd stashed in my gym bag. I didn't stop reading about the history of the Third Reich for a month. I realised his whole life had been poisoned, and mine with it. The ripples of trauma passing down generations, like

Shlomi had believed, until they culminated in Liat. I'd known that day at the age of seven, when I'd heard on the radio that Eichmann was in Jerusalem, that there was a darkness in the past I couldn't escape.

I stayed up all night thinking how it had happened and, to my mind, how it was happening in a different form again. Historians are of no help, psychologists barely, only God knows, because there's no line of reason that ends up requiring pressure chambers at Dachau, or flying planes of people into buildings, or killing a bus full of strangers. You were crying when you came in to find me pounding coffee at dawn still reading about the *Kinderaktions* in Lithuania: "Israel…you're obsessed. You're frightening me. Put the book down and come to bed. Put the book down. Come to bed. Come to bed. Stop that whistling. You'll drive me mad." I was whistling 'White Christmas' to fill the silence left by the radio that had run out of batteries. "You're obsessed by that song."

"At least you didn't sleep with Shalom," I said.

"Israel?"

"Yes."

"Nothing," you said. I glanced at a map of railway lines crossing the Baltic to Stutthof and into Southern Germany, passing the overcapacity to killing fields in Poland, and said, "How could he write it? I mean seriously. How?"

Your eyes had become smaller over the years, the bags beneath them bigger and darker. You were overweight, but it filled out your cheeks and made the bows of your lips plumper and more kissable. "How could who write what?" you said.

"White Christmas," I said.

"I'm tired, Israel. Listen to me, I don't have the energy to go through this again. I don't want to remember. I want to forget."

"I'm not mad. I want to know. How could he write a song like that?" I said.

"Why not? He was celebrating a new life."

"I'll give you millions of reasons," I said. "Could take us a year to get through their names. Got to laugh."

"Israel?"

"Yes?"

"I was thinking about Liat."

"They would have killed her twice. She's better off where she is."

"Oh, Israel," you said. "Come to bed. Please."

"Not until I understand. That doctorate got me nowhere. I've been teaching this for years. I've got nowhere. Give me a few more minutes."

"The words won't help. Let it lie. We can lie down together. Be thankful for that."

"Thankful?"

"Why are you bothered by it? It didn't happen to us. It happened to those poor people."

"It did happen to us," I said. "It always happens to us." You grabbed my hand and pulled me away from the book. "Okay," I said, realising I owed you back for your patience. We lay down in bed, and I fell asleep in the warmth of your armpit with the lyrics on loop in my head, "I'm dreaming of a White Christmas. Just like the ones I used to know".

When I woke up, you were watching me, and I pushed my lips to yours. We made love, discreetly, for the first time in years. Old people, but in the warmth of your body, I found happiness again.

The Big Jukebox, Hemi Rudner

I'd finally let myself go. My gut ballooned. A red T-Shirt I was fond of barely covered my belly. I quit the gym the moment young women started to resemble children. One doesn't grow old. Everyone else gets younger. A more wholesome reason for my weight gain was your cooking. I came back from lecturing to a table covered with stuffed onions and peppers, braised cauliflower, durum wheat parcels, and staples like eggplant with tahini, egg and parsley, or slow-cooked chicken and rice called *tabeet*, or *kitchree*, rice and lentils.

Your mythic past served up in a range of flavours, inherited memories bubbling and steaming in pots. Each bite, I got closer to touching your refracted soul, the smells you were brewing over the gas rings evoking the spice market at Taht-el Takia and the breeze from the slow-moving Dijla.[22] Certainly your journey into self, after years of resistance, was healthier than my going mental and talking to the dead in a graveyard. What was not was the sheer amount of food I could get down my throat. I put on ten kilograms in a year. Visceral belly fat, bad for the heart, good for the soul.

We'd wake mid-morning, after rolling about in bed together. You put an alarm on your Nokia phone to make me a *sabich* sandwich for my lunch at university. Although we'd stopped having sex, we were physically close through long, affectionate nights. Your cooking was fulfilling. Your body comforting. A second mother, the smell of your skin and sweat made me drowsy and content, so that, before your alarm went off, even if I was awake, I didn't leave the bed.

This recipe for *sabich*, I got by watching your clever hands, swollen at the joints, future arthritis not far away. Essential that the eggs are slow-cooked, from the Sabbath *hamin*, left baking overnight so as not to flout the commandments. For an unguent sponginess that goes with the texture and tartness of eggplant, salted and fried in olive oil. The tahini comes from a tub. Pour that on, much as you like. I liked a lot because I also sluiced on *amba*, mango chutney that made my feet stamp. The parsley lifts the condiments and the whole bite-full, with the addition of some sumac-sprinkled raw onion, is intense. We might have stopped having sex, but you found a new way of arousing me.

Your family had been part of the exodus of Jews, expelled from their ancestral homelands between the great rivers of Mesopotamia. Most from Baghdad, your father's mother was from Mosul. She'd come to Palestine and worked on a kibbutz, which is how your parents finally ended up in a moshav, unlike most refugees, who were shifted from transit camps to the rapidly growing development towns.

The Mosul connection was a meatier menu. At my pleading, you made *dolma*, minced beef cooked with rice, pomegranate juice, courgettes, tomatoes, peppers and grape leaves, and traditional skewers of mountain lamb, we got from a butcher in Ramle. Most recipes came from your mother, along with descriptions of starlit child-nights, the wafting smell of the tandoor, incense in the desert, stars licked by smoke.

That idyll, like my parents' childhood, was brought to an end by the ethnic cleansing of Iraq. Although, having made the journey here, your family seemed less anxious than mine, or me, for that matter. They didn't fear recurring genocide in the same way. You dipped your little finger into the pot.

"What about the *Farhud?*" I said, trying to whip up the indignation that plagued me, the same outrage and contempt for the world that served to keep my anger at full volume.

"What about it?" you said.

"Doesn't it upset you?"

"Of course it does," you said.

"So why don't you talk about it?"

"Because I'd rather not."

"Fine," I said.

"Taste this," you said, and spooned out a rich tomato sauce with coriander and *baharat.*

"Ooh," I said.

"Tasty?"

"Reminds me of my days in Yonatan's radio shop," I said. "I wonder what's happened to him. Probably dead."

"Stop killing everybody off. He's probably happily retired," you said. "No doubt you'll kill me off soon enough."

"Not you," I said. "Why did Iraq have a pro-Nazi government?"

"I don't know," you said. "Why did they?"

"I'm implying the answer with the question."

"I know," you said. "Everyone's a Nazi to you."

"Yes. From a Jewish point of view the fact that everyone's capable of being a Nazi means that they are. It's a safe assumption. Literally. Assume the worst, it will keep you safe. The fact that someone can be a Nazi in this world, even as a possibility, terrifies me."

"Let's change the subject," you said. "You're a broken record. Why don't you learn from your beloved radio?"

"The radio," I said. "At last you show an interest."

"Change the tune every now and again. Try selling me something that will make me happy for a while."

It crossed my mind that the Second World War began when the Wehrmacht dressed a brigade of German criminals in Polish uniform, mock-occupied a German radio station at Gleiwitz, in Upper Silesia, and pumped out patriotic Polish tunes on the kidnapped airwaves. The SS were dispatched to take back the station, and in quick time they slaughtered the fake Poles, and showed the gullible press the bodies as evidence of unjustified Polish aggression. I chose not to tell you this story, but I've found space for it now.

It continued to distract me that the German high command sought a moral justification for the total and pitiless destruction of a neighbouring country. The seizure of a radio station was imagined a satisfactory, imaginary premise. A radio station, a symbol of peaceful sovereignty, used as bait. Sort of makes sense to a radio fanatic like me. If someone were to take over Radio Tel Aviv, I'd seek their annihilation, because of what it prefigured.

Zoom out far enough, history becomes myth, further, it's nothing. Zoom in too close, you can't see it, pull out a bit and there's a coherent story one can make about the half-century before one's birth. It's a matter of getting the right perspective, the right time frame. Too far out and the story becomes meaningless, too far in, there's nothing to fit together, no pattern to make from events.

I switched on the radio, and you said, "By the way, do you need the boiler on?"

"Give me another bite." You cupped your hand under the wooden spoon. "Delicious," I said, sucking in air to cool my mouth.

"You don't need to have baths every day."

"I need hot water to clean the plates," I said.

"So, clean some plates," you said.

"That's not fair. I do."

"It's such a waste of money," you said.

The radio buzzed: "Give this big jukebox another coin. I want to sing a love song. I'm not satiated. And another coin, and another coin and another coin. And then we dance – ance – ance – ance – ance."

"Don't leave the boiler on," you said.

"Got it," I said.

"Don't," you said.

I got off the stool. Our new fridge had an ice-maker. I took out a Tupperware box of homemade chilli sauce. "Taste this," I said.

"It's too spicy for me. You exaggerate everything."

"You never try what I make," I said.

"Because it's always too spicy."

I'd bought a hand-powered food processor. I cleaned and cut chillies, parsley and two heads of garlic and ground it to flakes. There was a trendy delicatessen on Dizengoff Street that sold extra-virgin olive oil and artisan vinegars. On one of the bottles, a sketch of a bald man with an apple in his eye. I recognised him – "Arbel's Apple Cider Vinegar". I justified the purchase as a victory for me and my grandfather over the rules of the kibbutz we'd both flouted and were now forgotten.

I knew, despite kidding myself, that it was really a victory for the Arbel family. No one was sharing anything on the kibbutz anymore, and the Arbels had somehow managed to brand those trees their own. Tastes change over time. The vinegar was fruity and astringent and perfect for my chilli sauce. "The Arbels lived next to my grandmother," I said.

"Who?" you said.

"The thieves who made this vinegar," I said.

"Oh."

"It's good," I said.

"Can you turn the radio down?"

"My hearing's bad."

"It's so loud."

"I like this song," I said.

"Can't you turn your hearing aid up?"

"It doesn't work like that," I said, not sure if it did or not. "You know why the radio has to be so loud?"

"No," you said. "I've never met anyone who can spend so much time in a bath. It's too hot for baths."

"Unlike me, you can hear perfectly. But you choose not to listen."

"I've heard it all before, Israel."

"I wash off the sweat with a shower," I said.

"I know. Like there's no water crisis."

"I read they've solved that," I said.

Truth was, I didn't have baths more than twice a week, although the idea of me wallowing in a tank of heated water was so irritating to you that it must have seemed like I was permanently tit-deep in bubbles. Predictably, that evening, talk of baths got

210

me in one. "Keep the boiler on," I shouted, ice-cold vodka and grapefruit in hand.

"You're impossible."

I relaxed into the warm water. It wasn't just the boiler or my chilli sauce. Different ketchups, the brand of toilet roll, packaged or counter cheese, everything buyable became the push and pull of our personalities. You finding ever cheaper, bulk-buy goods and I ever more expensive prosciutto and other imported delicacies that filled boutique after boutique. I spent healthy sums of money on Grey Goose vodka. And stocked up on the Arbels' over-priced vinegar.

We argued over my need to use two Wissotsky teabags. The squabbles had an intimacy replacing, as they did, our tussles in bed. For the first time, we liked the same TV series, called 'All's Honey'. The semi-autobiographical work should have annoyed me given that it was such a thin simulacrum of the writer's life, but I enjoyed watching the heroine's relationship with her father, who had been a comedian when I was growing up. Had Liat been alive she would have been twenty-one and truly ensconced in the dating scene represented so honestly by the show. When I imagine Liat, it's somehow like she didn't have Down Syndrome. I see her at a bar being picked up by guys, and shiver.

I was so embarrassed sitting there with you when Yael's in a bar and an adman comes onto her with this: "*Take a visual. You're on all fours. Legs splayed. Nipples erect. I prepare my two thumbs and open your lips and concentrate on the sweet cherry. The sweet little ball. I'm concentrating only on him. No playing around. Focusing only on the cherry. Occasionally I give it a little tempo, but I don't move from the cherry. And so, I take care of you like I take care of you. You bend towards me, and beg, 'Yes, yes, enter me. I'm almost*

there, I'm already coming.' Then I get close to your ear and whisper,
'No. I want to take you to dinner'. We tried to laugh it off.

"Let's go to Bar Fly," I said.

"Come on, Israel."

"Seriously," I said. "Let's see what's going on."

"We're too old."

"No, we're not," I said. On the way, I calculated the length
of time we'd been living on Trumpeldor Street. At the bar, girls
were drinking large glasses of wine and wore skimpy vests with
tight jeans that, like leggings in gyms, hinted at a certain promise.
"Thirty-four years we've been here," I said.

"A lifetime," you said.

"Schubert was only thirty-one when he died," I said. "What
have I done in all that time?"

"Schubert again?"

"How are your parents?"

"They're well," you said. "Both in good health. For now."

"Good," I said, thinking of my parents' deaths. "Ah, that's
good." The cold froth of beer on my lip. You leant over and kissed
me. I raised an eyebrow.

"You deserved that," you said.

"What for?"

"For being happy."

"I've got fat," I said.

"Gives me something to cuddle," you said.

"You're a wonderful cook," I said.

"You're a good customer."

"You've lost weight," I said.

"Maybe I'm unhappy."

"Are you?" I said.

"You know," you said.

"Why?"

"It doesn't get any easier," you said.

"I know."

"That's why I like cooking for you. You're my baby now."

"Big fat baby," I said, and gulped at my Goldstar and felt that loosening of my shoulders, the bubbles massaging my back. I tilted my head this way and that. "Sure you don't want a drink?"

"I'm sure," you said. "I like watching you enjoying yourself."

"I'm having a good time," I said. "But still, what have I done in the last thirty-four years? Except gone mad. That was the highlight. The rest is static."

"You became an academic."

"I've gone on and on about the radio. That's for sure. Obsessed about the occasional song. Obsessed about the Holocaust. Taught all about the radio and the Holocaust. Lived in Tel Aviv. Listened to the radio while wearing a hat."

"It's different for a woman."

"Is it?"

"Of course," you said.

"How?"

"At least you're still alive," you said.

"What do you mean?"

"Fertile," you said.

"I was never particularly fertile."

"You could still have a baby," you said.

"No, I couldn't," I said. "Not with you."

"That's my point. Once upon a time, I was desperate to miss my period. Now, I'd give anything to see blood. It's an odd thing being an old woman."

"You're not an old woman."

"In that sense I am. Look at these young girls. Men don't look at me anymore. And they're right not to. I've nothing to offer them. I'm a husk."

"I look at you," I said.

"You do," you said. "Like a big fat baby. You stare at me. Baby boy. I don't know what I'm supposed to do with myself. Live out my life, but who for? I've only got you."

"Now *you're* killing us off," I said.

"I feel tired and worthless. I can't remember basic stuff. I sweat and am itchy all the time."

"The weather hardly helps," I said.

"It never bothered me before. You suffered from the heat. All pink and cute."

"Pink and sweaty. Not cute," I said.

"To me," you said. "My big baby. Take off your cap." I removed my baseball cap. "Blonde wisps, like a baby on a nappy pack."

"Thanks."

"No problem," you said. "Middle-age is a funny thing when you're childless. It's probably trying enough when you have children and a future. Life has gone on long enough for me to have got perspective on myself."

"We probably weren't meant to live so long," I said. "I've often thought Schubert was –"

"Really? Schubert?"

"Just illustrating my point."

"Thanks," you said. "You're always referring to Schubert as if he's your best friend."

"Sorry," I said. "He's a frame of reference."

"Don't apologise," you said. "We're both old and young, aren't we, Israel? Caught in the middle."

"We certainly have quite a past," I said.

"But a future?"

"I'm trying not to think too much." My second Goldstar came and I flicked the glass with a fingernail. It made a dull thud. "This stuff helps."

"No future, but years left to contemplate what might have been. I died with Liat."

"I know," I said.

"I wrote half your story. I came into that hospital. I allowed you to go crazy. I found our apartment."

"Why do all young girls have tattoos and dogs?" I said.

"I hate dogs."

"I love that you do. But don't tell anyone. I'm the only person that understands." She presented her knuckles, and I fist-bumped her.

"None of this waiting around is doing me any good. Look at these young girls."

"No," I said.

"Yes."

"Only you," I said.

"You need me," you said, lighting a cigarette. "I kept us together."

"I fell in love with you first."

"If it wasn't for me, we'd never have got together," you said.

"I'm not sure. Jung said that to understand ourselves we resort to myth-making."

"Back to psychology? I thought we'd got past that."

"I'm trying to make sense of what you feel," I said.

215

"I wish you'd write about us. You write well."

"How do you know?"

"I read your lectures notes. If only they hadn't been about radio."

"Come on," I said. "Let's put something on the jukebox."

"Jukebox?"

"Yeah," I said. "It's retro now. Can't you see? Young people are into irony. We've reached the end of civilization and they know it. There's nothing left to say. All they've got is irony." And out of the air came, like it so often does, an answer to my prayer: "And then we dance – ance – ance – ance – ance."

A young man knocked into my back and I spilled some drink onto my lap. "Watch it," I said.

"Sorry," he said.

"No problem," I said. You patted my hand. I stood up and, gripping you tightly, we danced on the pavement, with all the children and their tattoos and dogs and inability to communicate, staring at us as if we were representatives of the last generation that connects, the last generation where people listened, together, to the radio.

At university, like 'The Big Jukebox', I felt I was going through the motions, and my classes thinned out. There was no second Looly. Girls in the front row were made blue by whatever they were looking at on their laptops. In the middle of the year, I heard that Apple was bringing out a composite music player, camera, internet device and mobile telephone. I told myself that it was obvious the radio couldn't survive much longer and that, as I was getting old, I didn't care. But I did care. As the term ground on, the class got emptier. I'm not sure if harping on about the radio was my only problem.

Mention of the Holocaust seemed to make people uncomfortable. One girl, with a snide expression, said something I didn't hear. I wondered why people felt hostile about their own history. Perhaps they thought that the older generation was trying to trap them into feeling or behaving in a certain way. When I went through the list of names during roll-call I noticed a new pattern: Emily, Pierre, and Amy. Were there any Hebrew names left?

When I mentioned certain atrocities, they refused eye contact with me. What was it about reminding people of the great historical crime that left them prickly? It made it hard to teach my course. I wondered whether the Holocaust, like the radio, was becoming obsolete. Could facts, historical events, become so unfashionable, so unwieldy that people could simply dismiss them?

By July, the class was mainly third-year males who, having got lost on their way to engineering degrees, needed the easy marks I gave. They didn't have the artistic sensibility to see the radio in its rounded glory. Not one of them. They tapped away on their laptops, their faces that sky blue.

I was going through the motions, and the motions, when detached from anxiety about the future, are agreeable. I truly enjoyed brushing my teeth. Getting pleasure out of the boring stuff makes time slow. I'd ditched writing my 'History of Radio'. I wasn't insular or angry enough to write.

"I wish you'd do something," you said.

"Like what?" I said.

"When you were mad you burned like fire. Now, you sleep ten hours a night and two hours in the afternoon, and when you're awake…your eyes have a dreamy quality.

"You're funny," I said. "You used to find me funny."

"You were funny."

"I was mad," I said.

"But it made me laugh."

"And cry. You cried a lot," I said.

"It made me insecure. I did something stupid," you said.

"What?"

"Put salt in the sauce twice."

"Doesn't taste salty."

"Let's go to the cinema," you said.

The last time, we'd watched *Brokeback Mountain*. "When was the last time there was a decent film on?"

"How would we know if we never go?"

"I read the reviews," I said. "Nothing grabs me."

"Oh God," you said. You were right, my light. My life had been reduced to morning ablutions, midday feeding, afternoon napping, evening vodka, night-time feeding, midnight peeing. My head was not functioning much higher than a nurse for an ageing body, a body that required more and more attention to get through the day. When your body limits your potential through no fault of your own, you go easy on yourself. I certainly did not rage against my fading vigour. I patted my fat tummy as if I was nurturing something in there.

But your prompting worked. The next morning, I decided it was time to get my mind agile again. I returned to my favourite place to think and be melancholy, the Alice Gitter music library. It was a handsome spring day. The missile wars had abated, for the while, and I was looking forward to a quiet year of contemplation. But on what subject? I didn't want to write about the radio anymore. I wanted to write about what the radio meant to me. However, I didn't want to write about myself, not yet.

The library was warm, the settings on the air conditioner lagging behind the weather. I flipped through the compact discs and picked out a Prokofiev violin concerto played by Itzhak Perlman. I peered through the doors into the listening room. A young man with dark hair and thick lips with his head in his hands was bending over a book. I watched him for a while, and he didn't move.

The roof of the library was concrete and I imagined it could stand a direct hit from a missile, perhaps even a nuclear bomb, but would you be able to hear the siren and get under the table to avoid falling plaster? I thought it was not that long before the proposition would be tested. The young man put his hand out to find a can of Diet Coke he'd smuggled in. He reminded me of a young me, although we looked different. He had thick shoulder muscles that pushed out the T-Shirt he'd bought a size too small. There was a stain where he'd spilled some cola. He wore espadrilles, a hole where the big toe-nail had worn the fabric, and his right leg jigged up and down.

Next to him, a stack of CDs he was burning onto his computer's hard drive. Something about his hair didn't look Israeli. It was too long, but not long enough to be hippy. I thought he was probably French. There had been a lot of French people buying apartments on Ben-Yehuda Street and suddenly girls immaculately trousered with ballet pumps were promenading up and down the dilapidated pavement.

The young man crushed the can and ruffled his hair, leaving it standing. It was like he was trying to prove something to himself while also trying to concentrate on what he was reading. When I'd been writing my doctoral thesis, scoffing Lotus biscuits, I'd been unable to put pen to paper because of a similar nervousness.

I wished for his sake that he'd calm down and was about to tell him, when he got up, gave me an awkward smile and pushed past me. He had one wrinkle in his brow, carved in consternation.

I went over to his desk. He'd picked out hip-hop, jazz, and rock that I suspected was listened to by a distracted, unfocused, panicky mind. Folded down, by his laptop, a well-thumbed copy of *The New Grove History of Jazz*, open on Irving Berlin's entry. Pencilled notes were talmudically arranged round the text. I read a few scraps. Slowly, they began changing my impression of Irving Berlin, the man and the songwriter. "*At 5 o'clock on the morning of Christmas Day '28, his three-and-a-half-week-old son, Irving Junior, was found dead in his bassinet*". I remembered the photo Miss Weiss put on the projector, as I read: "*Those crowds of happy Austrians cheering Hitler into Vienna were hailing the death of their own culture*".[23] Then something that described to me why I loved jazz and the radio so much. It was, as it had always been, the remedy for the Nazi poison: "*Minstrels as a metaphor; for many Jews blackface was a code, one race's pain speaking for another. The Hebrew and the Coon. Minor third notes, the melancholy that's part of Jewish folk and Negro blues*". And then an explanation of how it fitted in with war: "*Berlin never forgot being a child in Temun, Siberia, when the Cossacks rode in and razed his village, sending his parents scuttling west. So about his adopted land, he had no doubts, and his were the words Americans turned to in the wake of September 11th*".

I felt guilty about thinking the worst of Berlin for writing 'White Christmas' during the Holocaust. I'd had a personal vendetta, since it had been playing when you'd tricked me about Shalom. I was also jealous that Berlin hadn't come to Palestine to write patriotic songs for us. The anxious young man was helping piece together who I was. In scraps in front of me, disjointed notes, an aleatory melody rearranged, a fragmented soul, discord into harmony: *"Twenty years later, returning by ship from a visit to London at the time of the Munich agreement, Berlin's thoughts were of war and love of country, and it was the latter he wanted to put into musical form. The 1918 version ran: Make her victorious/On land and foam/God Bless America/My home, sweet home. "I didn't want this to be a war song," said Berlin 20 years later. So, tweaking the melody and rewriting the lyric, he created a new ending: From the mountains/To the prairies/To the oceans white with foam/God Bless America. My home, sweet home"*.

Irving Berlin and I shared more than just our birth name, Israel. 'God Bless America' revealed Irving Berlin's true religion: homecoming. That's what happens when you haven't had one for millennia. God Bless Israel. I wanted to write something about my country, the country Shalom had died for, the country that you lit up, the city, the waves, the desert, the mountains, my family, my home, sweet home. I felt a rushing euphoria, like the waterfall outside Metula, I'd stared at with an open mouth, the water white with foam.

"Every 24th of December, while the rest of America was listening to 'White Christmas', the Berlins would explain to their daughters that they had some last-minute preparations to take care of, leave the house and, as the sisters found out many years later, lay flowers on the grave of the baby brother they never knew they had. When the girls grew up and left home, Irving Berlin, a symbol of the American Christmas, gave up celebrating it: 'We both hated Christmas,' Mrs Berlin said later. 'We only did it for you children'".

I emerged onto the plaza outside the Museum of Art, the Kadishman bronze goat-head squinting at me, and had the feeling that something big had happened, something I could explain.

I decided to do some prep work. You bought me a laptop, the one I'm writing on now, an old IBM, heavy and slow, but at the time a marvel. I could read the morning papers 'online'. The old hatred was back. I wondered how we were going to survive. "I can't believe it," you said.

"Come on," I said.

"What was her name?" you said. Your eyes darted about the table top trying to find it.

"I'm going to tell you."

"Don't," you said and wandered off, like you had when you were most sick, to spend the afternoon in the dark. When you came out later, you poured a glass of water that you drank in one go. Exhaling, and rinsing the glass, you stared at the running water and said, a couple of times, so that you wouldn't forget: "Liat. What's wrong with me? Liat."

Lost R The Days, Ninette

I felt momentary pity but, scratching my neck, promised myself I was going to wage war against them. There wouldn't be one left, buzzing around our apartment. Not only mosquitos but flies, I thought. I had to spray so their larvae wouldn't eat me. And moths, ants and cockroaches. The humidity was up to ninety-percent. My head felt like it might pop and melt down my chest.

I had a nasty bite on my temple where a mosquito had gone straight for an artery that fed my brow. The vessel pullulated in the heat. It wasn't far from my apartment to the grocery, but I was wet with sweat by the time I reached the bins halfway there. A cat leapt out of the refuse, and I put my hand onto the rim, and got hit by the smell of rotting food.

The strawberries were stacked high outside the grocery on Ben-Yehuda Street, where I'd come to get mosquito repellent and a plug that threatens to *"extinguish them all"*. The strawberries had been delivered from the Golan Heights, where in '73 my best friend was killed. I bought a box and two cans of spray. The repellent plugs had sold out. The mosquito Holocaust was going to be half-hearted. I sat down on the pavement and tapped the concrete with my palm. Without Shalom's sacrifice there wouldn't be strawberries mid-summer, the Golan's elevation providing a cooler climate.

I peered up at the hazy sky, white with moisture. I could feel it all around me, touching me. A scruffy, discarded *Israel Today* lay in the well of a palm tree. The biannual budget had passed. That's already too far ahead for me to get my head around. Will we be here in two year's time? How long can this city survive the heat? The sun's expanding, almost touching us. I'd read that morning on the *Mako* website that a jellyfish glow in the night was the end of the South Owl Nebula. The sun will swallow us – our little sun in a galaxy of a billion stars – or one sent sooner on the tip of a missile. The side of my big toe was swollen and hurting. Getting to my feet, I made my way to the pharmacy for the sixth time in a week.

"Insurance card," the server said. I handed it over and swirled my hands in a bin of discount lip-balm. She gave me a pissed-off look, and I withdrew my hands and whistled. She came back with a box of sleeping pills and scribbled with a biro and stamped her scribbles and gave me the pills with that look in her eyes.

"Don't worry," I said. "I won't be coming back."

"Thank you," she said.

I lingered in the air conditioning to get my blood temperature down before the trek home. There had been much talk of alien life after NASA had pictured a planet like ours. Obviously, NASA didn't get the cosmic joke, unfunny as it is. There's nothing out there. Out there is far too big and far too complicated for us to ever understand. We're inching forwards through infinity to an answer that isn't there. The gates of the cemetery were shut, but I could see, in the corner, organised through the Trumpeldor Memorial Fund, the plots I'd arranged for you and me, next to Liat. You were in the kitchen, playing with the radio. "Hot," you said.

"Not long now," I said.

"So hot."

"Boiling. It almost scalded my skin. Like steam from a kettle. Need ice," I said and picked a cube from the freezer and slipped it around my forehead. "Try this."

"Try what? Where did you get the ice from?" You looked confused and kept fiddling with the radio, going straight through the stations, without stopping, on a journey to something forgotten. "What am I looking for?"

"Weather forecast. Let's put the air con on and go to sleep."

"Okay," you said, but looked confused. I took an ice cube and rubbed it on your forearm.

"Come on then," I said, helping you up and across the room. There was a crackle on the radio like the one that saved my life. I pictured the wheat and maize of the Golan, rocks marking buried streams, granite piles and dormant cones, grey clouds filled with the sound of birds, chirpy as they killed insects.

"Wait," I said. I got the spray and filled the air. You coughed and waved a hand.

"Bring the radio," you said.

"What for?"

"Don't know," you said. "Might be useful."

"The radio's always useful," I said. "But it can kill."

"Kill?" you said.

"Shalom."

"Who?" you said.

"Shalom," I said. "Do you remember him?"

"Yes. How did it kill him?"

"Don't you remember the story?"

"No," you said.

"In the war," I said.

"There's always war," you said and, wavering at the entrance to the bedroom, your knees gave way, and I caught you by your elbows.

"Hopefully we'll be dead before they get another chance."

"Yes," you said, sitting on the bed and pulling your feet from your sandals.

"You're beautiful," I said and caught the sense of pride in your narrowing eyes as you recalled how beautiful you'd once been. I knew you could remember that. I was lucky you'd even looked at me. Wars go on forever. My whole life with you was shaped by one. My imagination formed by another. I grabbed your hands and looked deep into your eyes. "I have them."

"Enough?" you said.

"Enough."

"It's time," you said. "I'm forgetting myself."

"Ori?" I said.

"Liora, right? I'm Liora," you said.

"Ori, to me. Are you sure you want to do this?"

"Do what?" you said and smoothed your hand across the throw.

"Do this?"

"Yes," you said. "Before I do, I have to tell you something. Remember when we were outside that flower stall?"

"Yes," I said.

You tapped an arthritic finger on a sore knuckle. Your hands that had once fiddled with paper-clips. "You have to forgive me."

"Forgive you for what?" I said.

"I didn't say Shalom. I never said Shalom." You were losing your mind to a rare form of vascular dementia. You had visions and thought the street light the moon.

"Lie down," I said.

"Not yet," you said. "I never said Shalom. What was that music?"

"What music?" I said.

"The one you sang and later whistled." I guessed you were talking about 'White Christmas'. You touched my cheek close to my ear. "This one," you said. "This ear. The music was playing in the other."

"White Christmas?"

"Yes!" you said. "Sing it."

"I'm dreaming of a White Christmas, just like the ones I used to know." I propped you up with a pillow. "What's wrong?" I said.

"You didn't hear me. I didn't say Shalom," you said.

"What did you say?"

"Shlomi," you said. "He came over to collect your clothes."

"Ori?"

"I shouldn't have believed him," you said. "A week after it happened, he let you go."

"Ori?"

"Yes, Israel," you said.

"It's too late," I said.

"I know."

"I don't want to know."

"I had to tell you," you said.

"Don't worry. It's all behind us." You made a clucking noise. I put the radio on my bedside table. "Lies are a good thing. Berlin was right. White snow. He was dreaming."

"Israel?" you said.

"Ori?"

"Do you forgive me?"

"You're everything to me."

"I'm scared," you said.

"I'm coming with you."

"I want you to write something for both of us. Better than names on stones. Write something about Liat."

"I will," I said.

"I can see her," you said.

"Where?"

"Dancing."

"Where?"

"In a garden," you said. "It makes it easier to think, when I'm gone, you'll be sitting at the table in the living room on your laptop listening to your radio."

You'd said Shlomi. My whole life turned on this one fact and I said, "What about Liat?"

"The anxiety from the war," you said. "It was like you didn't want to get me pregnant."

"Liat?" I said.

"The war made her like that."

"Because of me?"

"Something went wrong. She was definitely yours."

"Mine," I said. "With her blonde hair and round head."

"Ours," you said. "How could we have let it happen to her?"

"She was perfect," I said and climbed into bed and switched on Radio Tel Aviv: "Your heart sends me dancing to the beat I love so. Don't say a word until your legs numb go. I'll tell my arms, catch you when you fall, tell my secret girl, you'll be the first to know."

"Don't cry, Israel."

The singing went on: "Lost are the days, fear in my bones.

Lost are the days, since you've been gone. Lost are the days, will you carry me home?" I emptied the capsules into my hand and fed you and you swallowed them with water that I tipped into your mouth and I held your hands until, in the tepid heat of the air-conditioned room, they were ice-cold.

When diagnosed, you said you wanted to die before losing Liat again, this time to the oblivion of dementia. I buried you under the willow, next to her, and it's time for me now. There's calm on the streets as the sabbath comes in and the traffic filters out, the odd taxi and nothing but pink, polluted twilight and a love song on the radio. I will take a knife, cut my wrists, lie down on the carpet and wait patiently to see you both again. My first radio was a present from my father on my seventh birthday with a lot of chrome knobs: "You can't touch the sky. It's impossible. Take this and listen to the invisible radio waves. They go on forever."

Endnotes

1   For reasons that should be self-evident, the German remains untranslated. Throughout the memoir Dr Shine shows an uncanny ability to recall speech. I should also mention that Hebrew names are kept in the original despite an initial experiment rendering their meaning in English. For instance, Shalom could be given as Peace. It felt contrived, however, and I ditched it. Some things are bound to be lost in translation.

2   Ori literally means my light in Hebrew.

3   Shani, for instance, means scarlet, and Schwartz means black.

4   Peace in Hebrew. Used as a greeting. Also a personal name.

5   Liora Shine's grave is situated by an oak. On one side of her, Liat is buried and there's an empty plot on the other. The only willow tree in the cemetery shades the gravestone of Raziella Ben Ari. Not a mimosa.

6   In Dr Shine's text he repeated the name Ori here. I decided to translate it. I hear him, you understand.

7   Very occasionally, I'm going to leave the Hebrew word in italics, when I think translation will affect the uniqueness of the rendering. Also, it's worth reminding the reader where we are. Israel. His name helps with that. But still, can't lose our sense of place. This is a translation, after all.

8   For some reason, the name seemed inauthentic to me. I felt unsure and went to the town council and asked for a list of drinking establishments on Ben-Yehuda Street in the late 1970s. I was lead

into a large, airy room, worthy of one of the great state-funded libraries in Western Europe, or even some European vanity project in Brussels, the likes of which distracted WG Sebald. In the middle of the room, at the point of the coaxial, sat Orly, a girl whom I had slept with the night before who had ginger hair that smelled of sugared butter. I was not surprised to see her (it's a small city), but also because she'd told me about this place when I'd mentioned to her my doubts about a location in a novel I was writing (I didn't have the heart to tell her I was a translator. Ask Freud. Writing gets you honour, power and the respect of women. That's why writers write. Translators are a nobler breed. They're interested in art for art's sake). I'd bumped into her at the Bar Fly, the night before. Although we'd just met, she spent two hours discussing her love life, which was less erotic than she imagined – some guy, a 'genius' she'd met at Shenkar, didn't get her. On the plus side, she did have a fantastic laugh when I managed to get it out of her. I suggested a game of making up pretend names for bars, something that was on my mind: Chocolate Bar, Bar Refaeli etc. The short of it is, and we spoke until the chairs were being stacked, I ended up the next day finding out that there was a place called Pub Lick in Ben-Yehuda Street in 1977. Moreover, I checked the names of all the subsequent places mentioned by Dr Shine and all are 100 per cent accurate, proving he had an incredible memory, except for trees.

9   This joke fortuitously works in both English and Hebrew because of the Greek etymology of the word theory.

10 Yonatan was apparently fond of quoting Ecclesiastes.

11 Need I mention that I know exactly what he was talking about?

12 The Hebrew phrase used by Dr Shine, which I translated as 'adefinable' is לֹא נִיתָן לְהַגְדָּרָה.

13 In other cases, I did go back and reorganise the chronology of his thought. In this instance, as he was drawing attention to it to say something else, I did not. Although, I only concluded this after putting in a scene where he kissed his mother on the lips as he got into bed with

her the night after he'd caught her having sex. It didn't feel right.

14 It's strange to me that it didn't occur to Dr Shine that the true meaning of his dreams about salamanders was that he was repressing the word and name Shalom, hereby substituting it for the Arabic salam, and that he and Ori's trouble with fertility as well as her likeness to Shalom meant that he mixed the Hebrew ending of the word 'andra', meaning a sort of man-woman. As a Freudian, I'd have thought he'd have leapt at it. Any deconstruction of the meaning of Dr Shine's words by him must come with a reconstruction of the meaning of the text by me, the translator. Shalom appears nowhere in this chapter. Because he has been repressed. That's the meaning of the recurring salamander dream.

15 In Hebrew this was חג המולד לבן which roughly translates as 'White Holiday of the Birth' so that it doesn't literally foreshadow Dr Shine's proposal scene, although I'm sure he was hinting at it.

16 Literally, 'to me you'.

17 This first paragraph is lifted in its entirety from the lyrics to Eviatar Banai's song, 'I've Got a Chance'. I found it hard to tell, for sure, whether he was thinking about the song as it played in 1997 and the emotions connected with it then, or whether he was relating to the song as it spoke to him as he was writing the memoir. Either way, the direct copying of this text indicates a deep emotional attachment to this song, which he discusses elsewhere in the chapter.

18 High-fives or a game of patty-cake.

19 Chaos before creation is called Tohu Va-Vohu, a sort of onomatopoeic reconstruction of the world before the word was sounded.

20 You remember that Dr Shine stopped on the way to Metula to put a stone on the Rambam's grave i.e. Maimonides. I only interrupt to point this out because as a translator sometimes I can't stand the idea of you missing something.

21 Buttery puff pastries filled with cheese, spinach, potato etc.

22 Arabic for the Tigris.

23 Steyn, Mark. *Broadway Babies Say Goodnight: Musicals Then and Now.* New York: Routledge, 1999, (75).